ONCE UPON A TIME IN AFRIKA

A Sword and Soul novel by

Balogun Ojetade

ONCE UPON A TIME IN AFRIKA

A Sword and Soul novel by
Balogun Ojetade

Meji Books
Fayetteville, Georgia

Copyright © 2012
Meji Books
MV media, LLC
Published 2012

This story is a work of fiction. Any references to real events, persons and locales
are intended only to give the fiction a sense of reality and authenticity.
Any resemblance to actual persons, living or dead is entirely coincidental.

ISBN Number: 978-0-9800842-3-8

Cover art by Stanley Weaver Jr.

Cover Design by Uraeus
Layout/Design by Uraeus
Edited by Valjeanne Jeffers

Manufactured in the United States of America

First Edition

AFRICAN UPLIFT

By Charles R. Saunders

Centuries ago, the philosopher Pliny wrote: "Out of Africa, always something new." That adage is as applicable now as it was then, as the new sub-genre called Sword and Soul continues to demonstrate. Sword and Soul is fantasy and sword-and-sorcery fiction, set in either an African or African-derived locale. One of Sword and Soul's purposes is to free Africa and people of African descent from the colonization of negative stereotypes that appear far too often in fantasy fiction —and just about everywhere else, for that matter. Another is to tell good stories that anyone, regardless of ethnic background, can enjoy.

Sword and Soul is growing fast, with my *Imaro* and *Dossouye* novels, Milton Davis's *Meji* and *Changa* series, Carole McDonnell's *Wind Follower*, Gregory "Brother G's" *Memnon* series, and the *Griots* anthology already available. Now, we have Balogun Ojetade's epic Once Upon a Time in Afrika.

The history, culture, mythology and folklore of the Motherland constitute a motherlode of inspiration for stories of all types, not just Sword and Soul. And within Sword and Soul itself, there are many trails to blaze, as well as innumerable branches that extend from those trails. The trail Balogun creates in this book leads to Onile, the Africa of a world that is —and is not—our own.

One of the most overlooked aspects of the Africa, of the world we know, is the vast diversity of the continent. Contrary to the "all blacks look alike" stereotype, Africa has— and has always had—a staggering variety of ethnicities, cultures, languages and landscapes. In *Once Upon a Time in Afrika*, Balogun encompasses the full range of Africa's variety, leaving the reader awed but not overwhelmed. Balogun doesn't hit us over the head with the wonders of Onile. He opens the door, then presents his rich and detailed setting in a way that allows the reader to immediately enter and engage.

Once Upon a Time in Afrika focuses on a hectic romance between a princess named Esuseeke (or Seeke for short) and a warrior named Akin. Their relationship develops within the situation of a grand tournament that attracts fighters from the length and breadth of Onile. The prize for which the contestants are to vie is the hand of Esuseeke in marriage. Akin is in the tournament—but not as himself.

In the context of the tournament, Balogun introduces a little-known aspect of African life: indigenous martial arts. A skilled martial artist himself, Balogun has studied the various fighting-styles native to Africa, and that knowledge shines through in the variety and intensity of his fight scenes.

There's more than just individual combat in *Once Upon a Time in Afrika*, though. A rival continent is bent on conquering Onile and enslaving its inhabitants. Armies gather. Sorcerous forces escalate. Doom looms.

Magic and mayhem. Gods and glory. Witches and warriors. *Once Upon a Time in Afrika* has all this, and much more. It is Sword and Soul at its finest, casting a long shadow over the "jungle lord" and "lost city" motifs that have previously prevailed in fantasy fiction set in Africa.

But don't just take my word for it. Read on, and see for yourself.

I Dedicate This Book:

To Milton Davis
*For pushing me to expand upon the world of Onile, to further
develop the characters, to give more depth to the description
of events, to give this novel wings and then let it soar. It is a
better novel—and I am a better writer—because of that.*

And to my Ancestors
*Who continue to show me our power, our beauty, our genius.
You are my blood, my bone, my heart.
I will continue to do my best to represent you well.*

CHAPTER 1

"She is fighting again!"

Temileke's narrow, leathery feet beat a staccato rhythm upon the hard, mahogany floor.

It would be so much easier to use the apere ayorunbo, Temileke thought. But the use of magic was forbidden within the walls of the palace.

As Baṣorun—Chief-Of-Staff and Prime Minister, in service to the ruler of the mighty empire of Oyo—Temileke *had* to follow the rules, although the avid collector of powerful magic items desired to do otherwise.

Temileke continued to scurry through the wide halls of the palace, alerting the Alaafin to his presence long before he reached the chambers of the King of Kings. To startle the Alaafin of Oyo was frowned upon. "Your Highness… Eṣuṣeeke is fighting again!"

Alaafin Rogba Adewale rolled his eyes as he broke off a piece of spicy-sweet akara cake and fed it to his Chief Wife, Usiade. "Your daughter thirsts for battle, it seems."

"*Your* daughter needs a strong husband to cool that fiery spirit," Usiade replied. "However, I believe it was the Alaafin, in all his wisdom, who sent his eldest daughter off to
be trained as a warrior instead of as a wife."

"Her birth divination told us that Ṣeeke needed a powerful woman to guide her through childhood," the Alaafin said.

"So, you send her to Oyabakin—the most feared warrior on the continent of Onile?"

"She is also a great healer, Usiade."

"The borrower who does not repay, finds no money to borrow," Usiade replied. "Oyabakin heals her opponents so she will have someone to beat up again later."

A light, tapping noise came from the door of the Alaafin's

chamber.

"Come in, Temileke," the Alaafin ordered.

Temileke entered the chamber and gracefully lowered himself into a prone position, with his arms at his sides and his forehead pressed to the floor. "Ekaaro, Your Highness," Temileke said.

"Dide," the Alaafin replied.

At the command to rise, Temileke hopped to his feet, belying his sixty-plus years of age.

"Who is Ṣeeke fighting *this* time?" The Alaafin asked. "A patron of the marketplace? An over-flirtatious priest? One of her schoolmates?"

"Her brothers," Temileke answered. "The twins—
Tayewo and Kehinde."

The Alaafin's full, jovial face twisted into a frown. "Their mother promised me I would have no more trouble from those boys!"

"Ajoke does the best she can with the twins," Usiade said. "But those boys are nearly as headstrong as Ṣeeke."

The right corner of Usiade's mouth curled into a sly smile. "Besides, the Alaafin has not given Ajoke that third child, who is destined to cool the twins down."

The Alaafin rolled his eyes and turned his attention to Temileke. "Do your wives give you as much trouble, Baṣorun?"

"I believe the Chief Wife is merely extolling the virility of our Great King, Your Highness," Temileke replied.

"Forever the diplomat, eh, Temileke?" The Alaafin snickered. "Well, let us go attend to my pugilistic offspring!"

CHAPTER 2

Tayewo sailed through the air, thrashing like a mackerel on the floor of a fisherman's boat. He landed on a row of large, wooden bata drums—his buttocks, elbows and the back of his head pounding out a thunderous tune before he slid to the floor. Tayewo grunted as his ebony-toned back smacked the cold marble.

Ṣeeke smiled. It was the first time she had thrown someone with a wheel-kick, and she had executed it perfectly. *Mistress Oyabakin would be proud!* she thought.

Ṣeeke's smile faded as she found herself hoisted into the air by her brother, Kehinde, who had trapped her in a powerful bear-hug from behind.

Although identical in size and appearance to Tayewo, Kehinde was nearly twice as strong and knew how to use his strength to do damage.

Ṣeeke hooked her left foot around Kehinde's left ankle and then reached behind her, pressing her palm into the middle of Kehinde's back.

Try as he might, Kehinde could not throw his sister, who seemed to be stuck to him like palm oil to white cloth.

Suddenly, Ṣeeke bent forward, grabbing Kehinde's right ankle with both hands. She continued her forward momentum, rolling over into a seated position, which sent Kehinde careening over Ṣeeke and onto his back, beside his sister, with his right leg trapped between both of hers.

Ṣeeke held Kehinde's foot tightly to her chest as she propelled herself backward, until she lay beside her brother. She then thrust her pelvis upward, against Kehinde's knee, as she arched her back and expanded her chest.

Kehinde screamed in agony as his knee hyper-extended and the ligaments stretched to their limits.

"*Release him Ṣeeke! Now!*" Ṣeeke immediately recognized the bellowing, baritone voice. "Yes, Baba."

Ṣeeke released her grip on her brother's ankle.

Kehinde rolled onto his side, massaging his aching knee.

"Is Kehinde's knee dislocated?" The Alaafin asked.

"No, father," Ṣeeke said, as she sprang to her feet. "He should be fine in a day or two."

"How does the knee feel?" The Alaafin asked Kehinde.

"It hurts when I do *this*, Baba," Kehinde replied, extending and then bending his knee in a stiff, choppy rhythm.

"Then, don't *do* that," the Alaafin said.

The King of Kings searched the immense room. Bata drums, talking drums and ṣekere were strewn about. Iron, silver and brass agogo remained in a neat row against the far wall. The bells were the Alaafin's prized instruments, used to call down the Oriṣa during festivals in honor of the gods and heroes of Oyo.

"Where is Tayewo?"

"Right here, Baba," Tayewo replied as he struggled to his feet amidst the pile of fallen bata drums.

"Ṣeeke, did I not tell you to refrain from violence in the palace?" The Alaafin inquired.

"Father…mother…this was not my fault," Ṣeeke said. "Tayewo and Kehinde started the fight."

Tayewo pointed a trembling finger at Ṣeeke. "That is a lie! Kehinde and I were drumming. Ṣeeke came in and began to dance…"

"And, as usual, her dancing was off-beat," Kehinde chimed in. "So, we stopped drumming."

"My dancing was *not* off!" Ṣeeke shouted. "Their *drumming* is so poor, it is nearly impossible to dance to. Who did you pay to teach them father? A deaf man with no arms?"

"You see, father!" Kehinde said. She insults us constantly. We have grown tired of Ṣeeke's mouth!"

"That is why we decided to teach her a lesson in respect!" Tayewo said, leering at Ṣeeke.

Ṣeeke folded her well-toned, cinnamon-hued arms

across her chest and smiled smugly. "The problem is...your fighting technique is as weak as your drumming."

"What?!" Tayewo shouted. "Ṣeeke, if you were not my sister, I would…"

"You would have been beaten even *worse*," Ṣeeke replied, interrupting him.

"Enough!" The Alaafin commanded. "Tayewo…Kehinde…go home!"

"Yes, Baba," the twins said in unison as they prostrated before their father.

"Dide," the Alaafin said.

The brothers stood and then walked briskly out of the room.

The Alaafin placed a firm hand on Ṣeeke's shoulder. "Come by the royal family shrines in an hour. Your mother and I need to sit before the oracle with you."

Ṣeeke kissed the back of the Alaafin's hand. "Yes, father."

Ṣeeke then embraced her mother, placing her head upon Usiade's shoulder. Ṣeeke inhaled deeply, savoring her mother's mango and shea butter-scented skin.

"Smelling me again, child?" Usiade giggled.

"You know I love it!" Ṣeeke replied.

"I know," Usiade said.

"I love you, too," Ṣeeke said.

"I know. I love you, too," Usiade replied.

"I will see you soon, Iya," Seeke said, as she headed toward the door.

"I will see you in an hour, my love," Usiade replied. "And please," she said, tugging at Ṣeeke's red, cotton ṣokoto— the shin-length trousers worn only by warriors—"wear a skirt, for once!"

CHAPTER 3

Ṣeeke walked through the Oja-oba, the grandest marketplace in the world, one befitting of its name: "The King's Market."

The princess took in the delightful sights, sounds and smells of the bustling bazaar. Stalls of varying sizes were all run by women, as the dealings in trade and commerce were the realm of the powerful matrons of the empire. Everything, from rice to elephants, to fetishes of minor magic, was bartered and sold.

The smell of pounded yam, grilled goat, egusi stew and banana wafted across the market. Ṣeeke inhaled and sighed, disappointed that she did not have time to stop and enjoy a snack of dried fish and fried melon seeds.

Striding briskly toward the palace—which towered magnificently in the distance—Ṣeeke frowned. *This walk home would be so much easier if I wasn't wearing this skirt!* she thought.

Ṣeeke looked down at the ankle-length, cotton skirt. While she loved how the rich, indigo color contrasted with the splotches of sky-blue that polka-dotted it, she could not stand the skirt's restrictiveness. If someone was to waylay her, she reasoned, she would be forced to rely on fisticuffs alone. Grappling would be difficult and kicks would be out of the question.

Ṣeeke preferred the functional dress of the jagun-jagun; yet today, she would sit before the oracle: not as a warrior, but as a woman.

"A warrior is not male or female, not lawful or chaotic, not aggressive or gentle," Mistress Oyabakin would say. "A warrior is whatever is appropriate for the moment."

Thus, Ṣeeke had donned the uniform appropriate for the loyal and obedient daughter of the king of the empire of Oyo: an ankle-length skirt with matching blouse and gele head-wrap, a necklace and bracelet of orange coral—marking her station as royalty—and sandals, made from the finest leather, embroidered with glass beads of orange, indigo and sky-blue.

In half an hour, she would sit before Baba Fafore—the diviner for the Royal Family—and learn what Olodumare and the Orişa, the Creator and the Forces of Nature, had in store for her.

She prayed it would include travel to exotic lands and good fights along the way. *That would be heaven on earth,* she sighed. *Heaven on earth!*

CHAPTER 4

"Why?" Şeeke cried. "Why now?"

"Şeeke, calm yourself!" Usiade ordered. "You knew that the time for you to marry was fast approaching."

"But, mother, there is so much I want to do!" Şeeke cried. "So much I want to see!"

Şeeke plopped down onto the plush, leather pillows that covered the floor and sat between her parents. Sitting opposite them, on a mat of woven straw, was the famed and revered Babalawo Fafore Falana.

Having been the trusted diviner for the Alaafin's family for over sixty years, Baba Fafore's word was irrefutable.

The venerable priest threw the opele—the sacred tool of divination, constructed of eight teardrop-shaped halves of odede seed, connected by a length of rope, with four seeds on the left and four on the right—onto a white silk cloth, which sat between his feet.

The divining chain landed with the top two seeds, on both sides of the chain, concave-side up and the bottom two seeds, on both sides, convex-side up.

Baba Fafore studied the opele's configuration for a moment, pulling at his beard with thin, crooked fingers. The whiteness of his beard made his dark face appear to be a beautiful blue-black.

"Irosun Meji," the old babalawo proclaimed. "The sacred Odu Ifa Irosun Meji has fallen. The sacred Odu Ifa Irosun Meji speaks."

Baba Fafore stared at Şeeke, studying her face in order to connect with her soul. Once the connection was made, the learned high priest began to chant the appropriate verse—out of more than a thousand—from the container of destiny called Irosun Meji, which was one container out of two-hundred fifty-six.

"Adeisi divined Ifa for Atapari, the head." Atapari was going to receive a cap from Orişa.

They said no one could wrest his cap from him without bloodshed!

It is impossible to have two caps!

"That is why those born under Irosun Meji will often find life a struggle."

Baba Fafore nodded his head and then interpreted the poetic verse's meaning for Şeeke and her parents. "It is imperative that Eşuşeeke marries soon. However, she cannot marry an ordinary chief or prince, as is normally befitting a woman of her royal status."

The Alaafin and Usiade exchanged glances. Usiade shrugged and then threw up her hands in confusion.

"Then whom, Baba?" Usiade asked.

Baba Fafore pointed at the divining chain. "Irosun Meji says that Şeeke must marry the greatest warrior in all the lands upon the continent of Onile."

The old babalawo stared at the Alaafin. "Your Highness, you must construct a grand arena and gather the best warriors from among Onile's children for a great contest of fighting skill. The champion will win the hand of your daughter."

"As far as I know," Şeeke began. "The greatest warrior in the entire *world* is my former teacher, Mistress Oyabakin. Am I to marry a *woman*, then?"

"Ifa says that while Oyabakin is, indeed, the greatest fighter alive, it will take more than fighting ability to be your husband," Baba Fafore replied.

"Yes, like a *penis* for one!" The Alaafin shouted.

"Rogba!" Usiade exclaimed, in shock at her husband's bluntness.

"Father!" Şeeke sighed, blushing.

The Alaafin shrugged nonchalantly. "Well, the warrior you marry must also be able to wield his *ancestral* sword if you are to bless us with many grandchildren, Şeeke!"

Şeeke rolled her eyes and hid her face in her hands.

The Alaafin drew a small sack from the breast pocket of his agbada and placed it on the white, silk cloth where the opele rested. "Please, take this gift of cowries for your time, Baba."

The King of Kings took Baba Fafore's hand in his and kissed the back of it. "Now, if you have nothing more for us, I respectfully request your leave. We have a tournament to put together!"

CHAPTER 5

The Emi Omo Eṣo—the young warriors who trained daily in order to earn a place among the Eṣo, the elite arm of the powerful military force of the Oyo Empire—sparred with wooden swords in the sand-covered Warriors' Circle, under the watchful and skilled eye of Master Gboyega Ogunlade: the Chief Teacher of the Emi Omo Eṣo and a veteran Eṣo himself.

Master Gboyega had fought and won victories in over a hundred battles, and was one of the instructors of the present Aare Ona Kakanfo: the Eṣo of Eṣo, powerful and feared Commander-In-Chief of the mighty Oyo war machine.

There was no warrior more respected in Oyo than Master Gboyega; except, perhaps, Mistress Oyabakin: his wife.

"Let your sword be an extension of your arm, your arm… an extension of your spirit!" Master Gboyega barked. "Lower your stances! More flow! More…*flow!*"

Gboyega deftly drew his mahogany practice swords from the sheaths on his back. The short broadswords whistled a low-pitched tune, as Gboyega twirled them in a quick and powerful figure-eight pattern. "When an Eṣo wields his swords or his spear, he is a reflection of the great Spirit of War, Ogun. When he wields his bow, he is a reflection of Ogun's brother,

the Spirit of the Hunt, Oṣoosi."

The young warriors stopped sparring and formed a circle around their master. Gboyega bent his knees deeply and brought his swords up to chin-height in front of his face.

"Akinkugbe!" Gboyega shouted.

A tall, athletically built young man, with cocoa skin, snapped to attention. "Yes, father!"

"Step forward!" Master Gboyega commanded.

Akinkugbe stepped forward into the center of the circle. He

faced his father and crouched into his fighting stance. Akin fought the urge to smile. He loved to spar— especially with warriors of the caliber of his father and mother —and longed for the day he would test his skills on the battlefield.

"Your opponent must *feel* the power of Ogun with each blow," Master Gboyega said.

The old warrior sprang forward on thick, heavily-muscled legs, swinging his swords with great speed and ferocity.

The swords of Akin and Gboyega drummed a fast rhythm, as Akin skillfully parried each slash and thrust of his father's weapons.

Master Gboyega spoke as he continued his onslaught. "Your opponent must *see* Ogun in the rhythm of your
    movement and the flash of your blade."

The old war veteran encircled Akin's swords with his own and then slashed outward, slamming the heavy, blunt swords into Akin's wrists.

Akin grimaced in pain as he lost his grip on the weapons. The young warrior's swords fell at his feet.

"And then," Gboyega said, pressing forward with a series of thrusts aimed at Akin's chest. "He will *taste* Ogun's iron in every wound you inflict! Aṣe?"

"Aṣe!" The circle of young men and women chanted.

Akin leapt backward and sidestepped, avoiding Gboyega's strikes. "*Aṣe!*"

Gboyega slashed downward, toward the top of his son's skull. "*Aṣe!*"

Akin spun to his right, evading the blow. Gboyega's sword sliced the air, just missing its mark. "*Aṣe!*"

Akin leapt toward Gboyega, his body rocketing through the air like a javelin. The top of the young man's head hammered into his father's solar plexus. Akin's Mohawk-styled hair flattened with the force of the blow.

Master Gboyega slid backward a few feet and then collapsed onto one knee. The Emi Omo Eṣo fell silent. They had never seen Master Gboyega hurt before.

"F-father?" Akin's voice shook with concern. He had

gotten carried away in the moment and struck with abandon.

"Akin…" Gboyega whispered.

The old warrior looked up. A broad smile was spread across his hardened, yet handsome face. "Akin has just demonstrated the power that Ogun grants us. Our swords…our spears...are just tools. *We* are the weapons! Aṣe?"

"Aṣe!" The Emi Omo Eṣo cheered exuberantly. "Aṣe!"

A sound, like distant thunder, joined the chanting of the young warriors. The ground shook and the scent of iron filled the air.

Master Gboyega leapt to his feet. "Horses approach! The riders are armed! Form ranks!"

The warriors placed their training swords on the ground around the Warriors' Circle, and then quickly retrieved their iron swords from a row of racks nearby.

Akin kept the twin, ironwood swords he carried on his back. The wooden weapons were given to Akin by his maternal grandmother, Efunlade. The swords had been used by Efunlade's father, Damilola, in slaying the last iron dragon, Garugu—a powerful and ancient malevolence that terrorized the citizens of Oyo for centuries.

Garugu ate iron and breathed the digested metal as a cloud of molten shrapnel. Thus, Damilola wisely chose to forgo the use of an iron sword and shield in favor of two swords carved from incredibly hard ironwood. The blood of Garugu was said to be soaked into the wooden swords, giving them nigh indestructibility and the power to pierce and cut through iron as easily as a lion's teeth pierces the flesh of a gazelle fawn.

The Emi Omo Eṣo formed two platoons. First Platoon was comprised of young warriors, hunters and blacksmiths who showed the desire and the potential to join the ranks of the elite. Distinguished by their red garb, the fifty men and women of First Platoon stood strong—a crimson wall against the approaching horsemen.

Beside them stood the thirty-two warriors of Second Platoon. With two years of daily training—one year in First Platoon and one year in Second—these young men and women were well-prepared to fight beside the Eṣo and, after proving themselves in a few battles, would earn their place among the seventy War Chiefs who formed the unparalleled Ẹṣọ.

Like the elite men and women of honor, courage and deadly efficiency they hoped to one day become, Second Platoon claimed indigo as their color: the color of Ogun.

The thundering of the horses grew louder. A dark mass appeared in the distance, at the edge of the Warriors' Compound. Gboyega recognized the wedge-formation of the horses and their rate of approach.

"It is the Aare Ona Kakanfo and his Senior Officers!" the old War Master said. "Emi Omo Ẹṣọ, salute!"

As one, both platoons dropped to their right knee, placing their right fist on the earth and raising their left hand to the height of their eyebrows, palms outward.

Master Gboyega centered himself between both platoons and assumed the same traditional warriors salute as those under his charge.

The Senior Officers of the Ẹṣọ were an awesome sight to behold. Each sat upon a well-muscled warhorse, which was cloaked in padded barding. The armor was buttressed with indigo-colored coral. Each member of the Ẹṣọ—a Balogun of either senior or junior status— wore the orange coral reserved for all Chiefs.

But as *War* Chiefs in the elite ranks of the Ẹṣọ, the indigo of Ogun was also required; thus each of the Senior Officers wore indigo-hued leather armor—studded with orange coral—which consisted of a helmet, vest, wristbands, ṣokoto and ankle-high boots.

Each Senior Ẹṣọ also wielded either a long bow and throwing spears, which hung from loops on each side of their horse's saddle, or a great spear and broadsword.

Grandest among the Ẹṣọ was the Aare Ona Kakanfo, a powerfully built man with cocoa-toned skin and a shoulder-length, braided ponytail that sprouted from the back of his, otherwise bald, head. The Kakanfo's station was indicated by his ojijiko, a cap constructed of red parrot feathers, and his apron of leopard's skin, upon which he was required to roost whenever he sat.

The Kakanfo wielded no weapon, save the *Invincible Staff,* a baton the length of a man's arm. Constructed of ironwood—and embroidered with orange and indigo beads in a complex zigzag pattern—the weapon granted the Kakanfo enhanced physical abilities and heightened senses.

Abe, the Herald of the Kakanfo called, in a rich, baritone voice from atop his horse: "Warriors, Olodumare and the Orişa smile upon you today! How do I know this, you ask? I know, because the Aare One Kakanfo is now in your midst! The War Chief of War Chiefs, the protector of the Empire of Oyo, Ibikunle Şangodele!"

The Kakanfo's warhorse trotted to the front of the Eşo's formation. "Rise, Warriors!" The Kakanfo commanded.

Master Gboyega and the Emi Omo Eşo sprang to their feet and snapped to attention. "Yes, sir!"

"Master Gboyega," the Kakanfo began, "it is always a pleasure to see you! I do not believe any army in the *world* is blessed with a better teacher!"

"Thank you, sir," Gboyega replied. "I do what I can."

"I have come to gather Second Platoon," the Kakanfo said. "We need a unit of light cavalry to join in the fight against the Urabi."

Master Gboyega nodded. "Second Platoon!"

"Yes, sir!" The Emi Omo Eşo of Second Platoon replied in unison.

"Gather your equipment and mount up!" Master Gboyega ordered. "I will inform your families of your promotion."

"Yes, sir!" The warriors of Second Platoon shouted.

The indigo-clad young men and women sprinted off, beaming with pride.

All, except Akin, who was held in place by the powerful grip of his father.

"Stay put, son," Master Gboyega whispered.

Akin shook his head in disbelief. "But father, I..."

"Stay *put*!" Master Gboyega hissed.

Akin snapped to attention and stood fast.

The Kakanfo smiled as he approached Akin and Master Gboyega. The Kakanfo leaned forward slightly in the saddle and pointed the Invincible Staff at Akin. The weapon glowed with a faint, indigo aura.

"What about your son, Master Gboyega? Is not Akinkugbe ready?"
    "Akin still has fundamentals to work on," Master
Gboyega lied. "He'll be ready soon."
    The Kakanfo's brow furrowed and his eyes became slits as he
studied Akin's and Master Gboyega's faces. His frown was brief, however,
and his brilliant smile quickly returned. "You know best, Master. Maybe
next time, Akin."
    "Yes, my Lord," Akin replied. "Maybe."
    The Kakanfo, Abe and the other Senior Officers of the Eṣo turned
from Master Gboyega and Akin and then rode off.
    Akin turned to face his father. The young warrior's handsome
face was screwed into a scowl. "*Fundamentals*, father? Really? I am the
best warrior you have! You *know* that!"
    Master Gboyega placed a firm but gentle hand on Akin's shoulder.
"Yes, I know. You are also my *son*, Akin, and I will not let my son serve
under a man like the Kakanfo!"
    Akin's eyes widened and his jaw fell slack. "The Kakanfo is a
great warrior…a wise strategist…a man of the *law*!"
    "He abides by—and enforces—the law to the point of insensate
cruelty," Master Gboyega replied.
    Akin lowered his gaze and swallowed hard, attempting to
dislodge the knot in his throat. "But the law…"
    "The Kakanfo is, indeed, a great warrior," Master Gboyega said.
"But he is not a great *leader*. You will *not* serve
under him!"
    "What has Kakanfo Ibikunle done to make you feel so
strongly about this father?"
    "He is a cruel man, Akin," Master Gboyega answered. "The
Kakanfo's obsession with the law makes him a very dangerous leader."
    Master Gboyega placed his right hand upon his son's shoulder
and, with his left, he pointed toward the earth. "Sit…I will tell you what
happened a few years ago, when Kakanfo Ibikunle came upon the tiny
village of Ijeti, in the Egbado Corridor."
    Akin and Master Gboyega sat upon the red-clay earth and the
seasoned warrior began to tell his son a story of cruelty, defiance…and
death.

CHAPTER 6

The village of Ijeti was at work. The men of the village pulled fruits and vegetables from the soft, reddish-brown soil. The older children filled baskets with the yield and the women carried the baskets—skillfully balanced on their heads—back to their modest homes of thatch and mud. Smaller children nursed from their mother's breasts or enjoyed rides on their mother's backs.

Overseeing the bustle was a hulking figure, who stood silently in the cool shadows at the doorway of the Chief's house.

The din of running hooves rumbled across the sky and made the earth tremble. The villagers stopped their work and watched the approaching horsemen as they drew nigh.

The hulking figure remained still. Silent.

Abe galloped into the midst of the villagers. The Aare Ona Kakanfo and the full force of the mighty Eṣo followed closely behind him.

"Citizens of the inimitable Oyo Empire," Abe shouted. "Prostrate in salutation, for your powerful and just Aare Ona Kakanfo—Ibikunle Ṣangodele—has graced you with his presence!"

The villagers fell prone, pressing their foreheads to the soft ground.

The hulking figure, however, remained hidden in shadow… watching.

"Rise, good citizens!" The Kakanfo said. His smile was warm and genuine.

The villagers rose to their feet. A village elder limped toward the Kakanfo. His skin was a mass of wrinkles on his thin frame. "How may we serve you, my Lord?"

"No, no. It is I who serve *you*…and your servant humbly asks for water for himself, his warriors and his horses."

The elder shook his head as he pointed toward a large,

circular wall of stones to his left. The wall was about three feet high and the stones were moist. "Unfortunately, our well has been a bit low. We barely have enough water for the village."

The elder then pointed to his right. "However, the village of Ifonyin—which is less than a quarter day's ride from here—should have *plenty* water for all of you. Our Chief, Oşogbesan, has taken some of the villagers there to trade and to bring back water for us."

The Kakanfo continued to smile although his piercing glare exposed his growing vexation. "The law states that if a warrior of the empire requests sustenance or shelter of a citizen of Oyo, his request must be fulfilled."

"I understand, my Lord," the village elder replied.

"However…"

"'However,' *nothing*!" The Kakanfo spat. "The water! *Now!*"

"I regret that *cannot* happen, my Lord."

The Kakanfo snapped his head toward the strong, bass voice. The forceful movement incited his pigtailed braid to dance upon his broad shoulders.

Standing a few feet away was the largest man Kakanfo Ibikunle had ever seen. The hulking figure had finally stepped into the light.

The man stood eye-to-eye with the Kakanfo, even though the Kakanfo sat upon the back of his warhorse. The giant's biceps were as wide around as a man's waist, and there appeared to be not even an ounce of fat on his heavily-muscled frame.

Adding to the big man's menace was his armor—his helmet was the head of a silverback gorilla; his vest, gauntlets and greaves were all forged from the fur, skin, and sinew of a huge silverback as well.

"And who are you, citizen?" The Kakanfo asked.

"I am Bamgbala," the gorilla-clad man replied. "Son of Chief Oşogbesan and protector of this village, my Lord."

"Well, my friend, *use* those muscles and fetch us that water, please," the Kakanfo said.

"Apologies, my Lord. I must deny your request," Bamgbala

replied. "My father will not return for a week…we cannot survive that long without water."

"You know the law! Bring me the water!" The Kakanfo ordered. "We will ride to the next village and I will send someone back with water for you in a day or so."

"I am sorry, my Lord," Bamgbala sighed. "We cannot."

The Kakanfo shook his head and then leaned forward on his steed, bringing his face inches from Bamgbala's. "We are *going* to take the water. Will you stand in our way?"

"If I must," Bamgbala replied. A hint of sadness was in the giant's voice.

Abe drew his sword and pointed it at Bamgbala's barrel-like chest. "Impudent dog! Then, we will cut you down where you stand!"

The Kakanfo pushed Abe's sword aside with the Invincible Staff. "Actually, Abe, he is an impudent *gorilla*." The Eşo laughed heartily.

The Kakanfo's smile returned as he leapt from his horse. "Eşo, I want all of you to stand down! I will deal with our apish friend myself!"

Bamgbala took a step backward. "My Lord, please. I have no desire to fight you."

"Killing me is the only way my warriors will leave here without that water supply," the Kakanfo said.

The gorilla-warrior nodded. "So be it, then."

Bamgbala closed his eyes and the eyes of the gorilla 'helmet' flew open. The gorilla's upper teeth sank into the top of Bamgbala's head with a sickening crunch as the teeth penetrated Bamgbala's skull. The giant let loose a roar that sent the Eşo's horses rearing on their hind legs and then—disregarding the commands of their Eşo masters—running for cover.

Bamgbala, now fully possessed by the spirit of the silverback, pounded his thick chest with his massive fists.

The Kakanfo continued to smile as he pointed the tip of the Invincible Staff at the ground. The staff's indigo aura glowed more intensely, and the earth shivered like a baby just out of its bath.

Bamgbala charged forward, his knuckles scraping the ground as he galloped toward the Kakanfo.

The Kakanfo slammed the pommel of the Invincible Staff into the ground and the earth rose in a massive, rushing wave toward the gorilla-warrior.

Bamgbala somersaulted over the crest of the earthen wave and then ran down the wave's body toward the Kakanfo. The giant shot out a powerful punch that struck the Kakanfo's chest like a cannonball.

The force of the crushing blow sent the Kakanfo flying backward as the air *whooshed* from his lungs.

The War Chief of War Chiefs tucked his knees into his chest, forcing air back into his lungs. The Kakanfo lowered his chin to his chest as he struck the ground. He rolled with the force, tumbling head over heels for several yards. The Kakanfo came to rest in a kneeling position and then hurled the Invincible Staff.

The weapon buzzed through the air, speeding toward Bamgbala like a missile. The gorilla-warrior lurched to his left, evading the weapon. He swiftly raised his thick, right hand and snatched the Invincible Staff out of the air.

Bamgbala clutched the Invincible Staff in both fists and then pressed his hands inward in an effort to snap the weapon in two.

But the Invincible Staff lived up to its name and did not budge. For all his power, Bamgbala could not harm a weapon carved millennia ago by Ogun himself.

The Kakanfo grinned triumphantly. He closed the fingers of both hands into tight fists and the Invincible Staff's aura grew in size and intensity, until it looked as if Bamgbala stood in the bowels of an indigo sun.

The giant roared in agony as his insides expanded in unison with the Invincible Staff's aura. He tried to drop the weapon, but the Invincible Staff was now fused to his hands.

Bamgbala's roar diminished to a whimper as his bones, his organs and his muscles stretched to their limit. A loud, popping sound escaped Bamgbala's chest and then he exploded inside his skin.

The gorilla-warrior's flesh collapsed to the earth with a moist *flump.*

The Invincible Staff rose from the mass of flesh, fur and gore and flew into the Kakanfo's extended palm.

"The law *will* be abided by!" The Kakanfo shouted at the terrified villagers. "Now, fetch me that *water*!"

CHAPTER 7

Akin sat in silence for a moment. His throat was dry— he could barely swallow—and he felt as if a hole had been bored into his gut.

"I understand, father," Akin said with a weak nod.

Master Gboyega jumped to his feet. "Good! Your time to prove yourself will come soon enough."

The master grabbed his son by his wrists and pulled the young man to his feet. "Now, go feed the horses and then sweep the Kakanfo's ile. I'll see you at home when you're done."

"Yes, sir!" Akin replied.

Gboyega watched his son turn and jog toward the stables. The old warrior then turned and headed home for a hot meal and a warm embrace—both courtesy of his beloved Oyabakin.

Master Gboyega slapped himself in the forehead. "I promised to bring home a few yams," he sighed. The master turned around and headed north toward the marketplace.

The winding road led past the palace wall where several craftsmen were busily carving the history of the Alaafin's ancestors into it.

Master Gboyega continued on until he noticed someone lying face-down a few yards up the road. The veteran warrior sprinted toward the person. "What is wrong, friend? Can you hear me citizen?"

The stranger did not respond.

Master Gboyega crept closer. It was a young man. His eyes were closed, and his chest rose and fell in quick, erratic bursts.

"Brother, can you hear me? Are you conscious?" Master Gboyega asked.

The man's eyes sprang open and a sideways smile stretched across his angular face as he rolled over onto his back. "Of course I am, old man."

Master Gboyega felt the point of a knife at his throat.

"Your money, or your blood!" the man demanded.

"I have no money and my blood is weak and runs slowly—hardly worth taking," Master Gboyega replied.

"What?! Are you toying with me, you old fool?" The man spat. "Meet my demands or I will…!"

Master Gboyega drove his thumbs into the young man's armpits.

The young man's eyes rolled back in his head and his jaw fell slack. His eyes closed and his head fell limply to the side.

Master Gboyega slid the knife out of the would-be robber's palm. He inspected it. The handle of the keen, iron blade was constructed of smooth, red marble and a large ruby was set into the pommel of the weapon.

Nice knife! This will make a wonderful gift for Oyabakin! Master Gboyega slipped the knife into a pocket in his vest, rose and continued on, toward the marketplace.

CHAPTER 8

Ṣeeke touched her forehead to the floor at the foot of the royal shrine to Oṣoosi, brother of Ogun: the Oriṣa of archery, the hunt, tracking and riches—as she did every morning.

In return for Ṣeeke's loyalty and diligence, Oṣoosi had blessed her with uncanny accuracy and speed with a longbow. And Ṣeeke was known throughout the Oyo Empire as an archer without equal.

Ṣeeke rose and walked backward out of Oṣoosi's shrine, which was painted with alternating diagonal stripes, in the Hunter-Oriṣa's sacred colors of blue and yellow.

Whispers echoed throughout the ten spherical edifices that comprised the royal Oriṣa and Ancestral shrines.

Ṣeeke crouched low and crept around the buildings, until she located the source of the voices—the red and white sphere that housed Ṣango, the Oriṣa of thunder, lightning, courage and rainfall.

The princess recognized one voice that emanated from within the shrine: Alaafin Rogba Adewale, her father. "So, that is the situation, Abe," the Alaafin said. "Please, inform the Aare Ona Kakanfo as soon as you can."

"A tournament of this magnitude sounds very exciting, Your Highness!" Abe replied. "The Kakanfo will be pleased."

"And I am sure he will be the one to win my daughter's hand in marriage," the Alaafin said. "I do not know of *any* man who can defeat the Kakanfo!"

"In combat—man-to-man—the Kakanfo is unequaled, Your Highness," Abe whispered.

We'll see about that! Ṣeeke thought, as she crept away from the royal shrines. *The Kakanfo may be unequaled in 'man-to-man' combat, but let's see how he fares in* woman-*to-man combat!*

* * *

Akin swept the dust from the floor of the Kakanfo's armory, admiring the War Chief of War Chief's sizable collection of suits of armor, swords, axes, spears and shields— all of the finest craftsmanship.

The armory's centerpiece, which sat upon an ivory podium, was the Kakanfo's ceremonial crown constructed of hardened leather, with white and indigo beaded embroidery. The crest of the conical crown was in the form of a white bird with an indigo head and beak. The front of the crown ended in a white veil of indigo and white glass beads.

As Akin busily whisked the capacious room, he sang his favorite song, a lively tune in praise of the Divine Trickster, Cosmic Law-Enforcer and Keeper of Aṣe: the Oriṣa, Eṣu.

"Latopa, latopa
Eṣu gang-gang
Latopa, latopa
Eṣu gang-gang
Olomope mi fa ye
Eṣu gang-gang
Olomope mi fa ye
Eṣu gang-gang
Olomope mi fa ye bobo
Eṣu gang-gang"

Akin danced as he swept and sang, bending slightly forward at the waist, hiking his buttocks up comically and dancing on one foot in mimicry of Eṣu's movements.

Akin danced and swept toward the center of the room. Lost in the spirit of Eṣu, Akin was unaware of how close to the Kakanfo's crown he had gotten. Suddenly, his buttocks bumped against the stand upon which the crown rested.

The ornate crown teetered for a moment and then toppled off its stand.

Akin spun quickly toward the crown and caught it in his trembling hands just before it struck the ground.

Akin stared at the beautiful, ornate crown and a sly smile spread across his face.

Filled with Eṣu's mischievous and playful energy, Akin slipped the crown over his Mohawk-styled hair and placed it on his head. The veil fell over his face and, although his countenance was completely hidden from view, Akin was able to see as clearly as if the veil was not before his face. Such was the aṣe of the crowns of the Oyo Empire, which were crafted by the most powerful wizards and witches in Onile.

Akin stood with his legs wide apart, his chest thrust forward and his fists upon his hips. "I am the all-powerful Aare Ona Kakanfo! Commander-In-Chief of the fearsome warriors of Oyo! Unbeatable... unbreakable..."

"And *unquestionably* full of himself!"

Akin whirled around toward the husky, alto voice.

Standing before him was the most beautiful woman he had ever laid eyes upon, which was saying much, because the Oyo Empire held many fine distractions for a man.

Akin had seen the woman once before, when they were both much younger. He had stealthily followed his mother to the palace and snuck into the training hall, where the beauty before him took private instruction from the great Oyabakin.

"Princess Eṣuṣeeke," Akin began. "To what do I owe the honor of your presence?"

"So you are the mighty Aare Ona Kakanfo," Seeke said, looking Akin up and down.

Akin knew the consequences of wearing another man's or woman's crown—particularly one of as lofty a station as the Aare Ona Kakanfo. Having no desire to be hanged or to be drawn-and-quartered, Akin decided to keep up the façade. "Umm...yes, I am."

"I understand that you are a good fighter," Ṣeeke said.

"The best!" Akin replied.

Ṣeeke crossed her arms on her chest. "Would you mind backing that claim up?"

"Against whom?" Akin asked.

"Me," Ṣeeke answered.

Akin buckled over with laughter.

Ṣeeke continued to stand with her arms crossed, staring at Akin with a raised eyebrow. Her expression was like stone.

"Are you serious?" Akin chuckled. He removed the Kakanfo's crown and returned it to its podium.

"I am," Ṣeeke replied.

"Why do you want to fight *me*?" Akin inquired.

"There is a tournament coming up," Seeke began.

"The champion is supposed to win my hand in marriage. My father is sure that *you* will be that champion. *I* have my doubts."

"Why do you doubt?" Akin asked.

"My father is a great king, but he is no warrior," Ṣeeke said. "His skill is in politics. He probably desires a marriage between us to ensure that you never rise up against him."

"The Commander of the entire armed forces of the empire could be a threat if he should develop political aspirations," Akin said. "That is why no warrior is allowed to live near the palace and can only enter it with permission from the Alaafin. So, your father is quite safe, Princess."

"Regardless, his fear or respect for your fighting skill is based on hearsay, not on his experience as a warrior," Ṣeeke said.

"Hmm…this tournament sounds…intriguing," Akin said. "The prize seems worth the effort…but, what would I gain by fighting you?"

"Defeat me and I will insist on marrying you—whether you win the tournament or not," Ṣeeke answered. "However, if *I* win, you must refuse to enter the tournament."

"You are stupid, crazy or overconfident," Akin said. "Which one is it?"

"I have *never* lost a fight," Ṣeeke said, thrusting her chest forward and lifting her chin. "My teacher was the great warrior and healer, Oyabakin. Do you know her?"

"I know *of* her," Akin lied. "Okay, let's do it!"

"Thank you, my Lord," Şeeke said, bowing her head.

Akin walked to the door and opened it. Şeeke sauntered past him and walked outside. Akin admired her athletic body as she walked by.

"You are beautiful and strong," Akin said. "You will give birth to children that will make me proud."

Şeeke assumed a low stance, with her fists raised to the height of her chin. "When I am done here, it will be *you* who screams in the birthing chamber!"

Akin smiled and dropped low into his fighting stance. "Come on, then!"

Şeeke skipped forward and whipped an arcing left round-kick toward Akin's ribs.

Akin shifted to his right as he lifted his right knee.

Şeeke and Akin crashed shin-to-shin. Şeeke winced and a low grunt escaped her lips.

Akin's smile widened.

Akin torqued his hips to the left and thrust his heel into Şeeke's supporting, right leg before she could retract her left.

Şeeke's right leg buckled and she collapsed onto her right side with a loud thud. Akin coiled his back and bent his

knees deeply.

Şeeke rolled backward as Akin exploded high into the air. Akin soared toward Şeeke. He drew his fist back to his ear as he descended upon her.

Şeeke pulled herself up into a handstand, drawing her knees toward her chin. As Akin came down on Şeeke, the princess thrust both feet into his solar plexus.

Akin stumbled backward, gasping for air.

Şeeke sprang to her feet and then leapt toward Akin, launching a powerful knee strike at his chin.

Akin shifted his weight onto his right leg as he thrust his right elbow downward, driving the point of his elbow toward Şeeke's thigh.

The force of Şeeke's upward knee collided with the force of Akin's downward elbow, crashing at the nerve plexus in the middle of

Ṣeeke's thigh.

The princess' eyes rolled back into her head and her legs spasmed as a purple bruise formed just above her knee and radiated up her thigh.

Ṣeeke's body stiffened and then, a moment later, went limp. She collapsed, unconscious, at Akin's feet.

* * *

Ṣeeke awakened moments later.

Akin stood over her. A brilliant, toothy grin was spread across his face.

Ṣeeke pulled herself to her knees. She lowered her gaze, hiding tears, which formed in the corners of her eyes. "Great match. I…I will honor our agreement and insist upon our marriage."

Akin slid the tips of his fingers under Ṣeeke's chin and gently raised her head. He wiped the tears from her cheeks with the back of his hand. Ṣeeke smiled weakly.

"As the victor, I wish to change the terms of our agreement," Akin said, as he helped Ṣeeke to her feet. "I want to spend time with you in order to learn more about you."

Akin walked back to the Kakanfo's house, stopping in the doorway. He looked over his shoulder at Ṣeeke. "If I determine that you are worthy of *my* hand in marriage, then I will simply defeat all the others in the tournament. If, however, I deem you *un*worthy, I will not enter the tournament."

Ṣeeke bowed her head. "The Kakanfo is too kind. I will leave you now, my Lord."

"Tomorrow morning, then," Akin replied. "Please, arrive early, Princess."

Ṣeeke walked away briskly, not wanting Akin to see the smile on her face and the redness in her cheeks.

"Tomorrow, my Lord."

CHAPTER 9

The setting sun cast a red hue over the Ogunlade Compound. Akin and Master Gboyega sat in the courtyard at a small, circular table of hand carved iroko.

Before them was a large bowl of egusi stew and pounded yam. The men devoured the food, dipping handfuls of the soft yam into the spicy stew and enjoying large bites.

Oyabakin exited the house carrying a steaming plate of barbecued chicken. Akin smiled as he watched his mother move. She was more graceful and lithe than most women half her age.

Like the Orişa Oya, after who she was named, Oyabakin was both a beautiful, loyal wife and a deadly warrior. Three hundred fights and never a loss, outdoing even *her* mother: the famed "White Warrior" of Itase Hill, Efunlade.

Mistress Oyabakin sat with her husband and son and began to eat. "The food is delicious, as always, my love," Master Gboyega said.

"Mo dupe," Mistress Oyabakin replied, thanking him. "The hens were young ones, from Oriyomi's farm. They are very tender."

"Tender, indeed," Akin said, sinking his teeth into a barbecued chicken breast. "Spicy…sweet…delicious!"

"Mo dupe," Oyabakin said.

The martial arts mistress studied her son's face as he ate. "Did you hear about the Grand Warriors' Tournament, Akin? The Alaafin is inviting the greatest warriors throughout the continent of Onile!"

"Umm…I think I might have heard something about it, Iya," Akin replied.

"The winner marries the Alaafin's daughter, Eşuşeeke," Oyabakin said. "She was my pupil for a few years. Very talented. Pretty, too!"

Master Gboyega rolled his eyes. "Oyabakin! Let the boy eat

in peace!"

"I am only mentioning it because I believe Şeeke would make a good wife for Akin," Oyabakin replied. "And I'm *sure* Akin can win the tournament."

"I'm sure he can too," Master Gboyega said. "It could be a good move, son. I've *seen* Şeeke…"

A dreamy expression came to Gboyega's face and the corners of his mouth curled up into a mischievous smile. "Woo…I might enter that tournament myself!"

A loud crack echoed throughout the courtyard. Master Gboyega's head retreated between his shoulders—like a turtle retracting into its shell—in an attempt to avoid another stinging smack on the back of the head from Oyabakin's hand.

"I believe the Alaafin is looking for the *best* warriors, not the most delusional," Oyabakin said.

Akin burst out laughing.

Another loud crack echoed throughout the courtyard. *Akin's* head retreated between his shoulders in an attempt to avoid another stinging smack on the back of the head—from Gboyega's hand.

"So, are you entering the tournament or not, son?" Oyabakin asked.

"I do not think so, mother," Akin lied. "You see, I…umm…"

The bowls and plates on the iroko table began to shake as a distant thunder disturbed the still air.

The three warriors stepped away from the table. Akin grabbed a chicken drumstick and ate it as he watched the horizon. A carriage, drawn by four horses, came into view. Flanking the carriage on each side were three horsemen.

As the carriage drew nearer, Akin recognized the mahogany carriage, with its gold inlay, as the carriage of the Alaafin and the horsemen—who were all dressed in red, leather armor—as his personal guard, the Ilari.

Akin swallowed nervously and made a silent prayer to the Orişa that Şeeke was not accompanying the Alaafin. Akin and his parents knelt in the traditional warriors' salute as the carriage and the horsemen came to a stop before them.

The door to the carriage swung open.

Beads of sweat rolled down the back of Akin's neck. His breathing grew shallow and his gut turned somersaults.

The Alaafin stepped down from the carriage. No one followed him out of it. Akin breathed a sigh of relief.

"Please, stand," the Alaafin said. "How are you, my dear, old friends?"

"We are well, Your Highness," Master Gboyega said, rising to his feet.

"How may we serve you, Your Highness?" Oyabakin asked.

"Mistress Oyabakin, I have need of your herbal knowledge," the Alaafin replied. "May I speak with you in private?"

"Certainly, Your Highness," Oyabakin said, pointing toward her house with her hand. "Right this way."

"What do you think is wrong, Baba?" Akin whispered. "Constipation?"

"Maybe," Master Gboyega replied.

* * *

Oyabakin and the Alaafin stood in the foyer of the house. The Alaafin inhaled, enjoying the nutty-sweet smell of palm oil as it burned in small, clay lamps that were placed around the house.

The palace was illuminated by magic, floating orbs of light that dimmed and intensified at his command. Convenient, yes, but he did miss the scent and warmth of a palm—or peanut —oil lamp.

"So, what is wrong?" Oyabakin asked. "Constipation?"

"No, no. Nothing like that," the Alaafin said, shaking his head. "In truth, it is not your skills as an herbalist I am in need of."

Oyabakin's right eyebrow rose as she glared at the Alaafin suspiciously. "What is it that you need, then?"

"In two seasons, the greatest warriors in all Onile will gather in Oyo for a grand tournament," the Alaafin said.

"Yes, I know," Oyabakin said. "Everyone in the marketplace

is talking about it."

The Alaafin looked around the room as if to ensure no one else was within earshot. He moved his face close to Oyabakin's ear and whispered: "I want you to enter the tournament and eliminate the Aare Ona Kakanfo's

competition."

Oyabakin stumbled backward, her eyes wide, as if she had been slapped in the face. "You want me to *what*?! I don't know if you've noticed, but I *am* a woman! I cannot…"

"You can *disguise* yourself as a man," the Alaafin said, interrupting her. "This can work!"

Oyabakin placed a gentle hand on the Alaafin's shoulder. "Alaafin Rogba, please, sit down. I can treat whatever it is that ails you."

"I am not ill; nor am I insane!" The Alaafin hissed. "The competition in the tournament will be tremendous. "There *is* a slight chance that the Kakanfo might lose in the Finals. However, there is *no* chance of *you* losing, so if you fight your way into the Finals and then *happen* to lose to the Kakanfo…"

"That is *cheating*, Your Highness!" Oyabakin spat. "I cannot…I *will* not take part in it!"

"Please, Mistress Oyabakin," the Alaafin pleaded. "A warrior of the Oyo Empire *must* be champion! Your people need you!"

"*You* need me—to cheat!" Oyabakin replied.

Mistress Oyabakin stomped towards the front door and snatched it open. "I want no part of your politics, Your Highness! I absolutely will not do it!"

"If you do, I'll make your husband Commander of the Palace Guard and build you a new compound next to the palace!"

Oyabakin closed the door. She looked over her shoulder at the Alaafin. Her lips curled up into a wry smile. "So…*how* many warriors do I have to defeat?"

CHAPTER 10

Akin stood in the doorway of the Kakanfo's house. The cool, early morning breeze blew his white, lace buba against his muscular torso. The rich material caressed his skin like a woman in love. *I will be sure to borrow garments from my father's closet more often!* Akin thought.

Ṣeeke strolled up the trail. Her shapely, well-toned body moved with feline grace and power under her yellow, cotton dress. Her toes were adorned with rings of amber and gold and her intricately plaited hair, which fell to her shoulders, was decorated with tiny fans, forged from brass.

To Akin, Ṣeeke appeared to be the embodiment of Oṣun: the Oriṣa of beauty and love.

"Ekaaro," Ṣeeke greeted Akin, smiling.

"Yes, it is indeed, a good morning," Akin replied. "Come on in."

Ṣeeke followed Akin into the house and to the main room, where Akin had prepared a table with several calabashes all filled with fruits from the Royal Orchard. Only those with royal blood, or with special permission from the Alaafin, were allowed to enter the Royal Orchard, which was a vast span of fruit trees and vegetable gardens commissioned by Akin's paternal grandmother—Oṣabiyi—a hundred years ago.

The Royal Orchard was home to Iginla, "The Great Tree," the progenitor of all trees in Onile. Iginla was considered to be an Oriṣa, and the bark and leaves of the mighty tree held amazing healing properties. It was rumored that the Invincible Staff of the Kakanfo was carved from one of Iginla's roots.

"You look stunning," Akin said.

"Mo dupe," Ṣeeke replied, blushing. "You look…not unpleasant yourself."

Akin laughed. "Always the warrior, eh?"

"Well, of course," Ṣeeke replied.

"Do not deny the well-formed woman that you also are," Akin said. Ṣeeke lowered her gaze and smiled.

"Please, sit down," Akin said. "Enjoy the fruits. I picked them myself."

Ṣeeke sat at the table and picked a small, sweet banana from the nearest calabash. "Impressive."

"Yes, it is, isn't it?" Akin boasted.

"Please, my Lord, do not be so modest!" Ṣeeke chuckled.

"I am often complimented on my incomparable humility," Akin quipped.

Ṣeeke laughed. "You are *so* sure of yourself!"

"The only thing I am sure of…" Akin began as he sat beside Ṣeeke. "Is that you are the most magnificent woman I have ever laid eyes upon."

Ṣeeke smiled, but said nothing. Akin and Ṣeeke enjoyed their fruit in silence; giggling, as they perused each others' blushing faces.

CHAPTER 11

The air hissed in protest as it was rent asunder.

The Başorun, Temileke, stepped through the wounded atmosphere onto the border of the farming village of Ijeti.

Temileke had acquired the apere ayorunbo—a powerful fetish that allowed its wielder to step sideways in time, thus teleporting instantaneously to wherever he commanded—from a venerable witch in Ile Aje, "the City of Witches," in exchange for the hand of his son as her consort.

Although the Başorun's son had initially protested marrying a woman three times his age, he was now rich, powerful and happy.

Temileke had not come to Ijeti alone. A tall, rotund, effeminate fop minced through the tear in the sky.

Temileke shook his head. The presence of the eunuch sickened him. Temileke would not dare give voice to his sentiments in the presence of the eunuch, however. For Jalili, as the morbidly obese man was called, was a deadly assassin and former Chief Guardian of the Emir of the Urabi, Nation of Urabin.

Jalili had followed his friend and confidant, Jabbar the Demon—former High General of the Emir's armed forces— from a life of service to the Emir, to a life of riches and adventure as freelance assassins and mercenaries.

"Your target is Chief Oşogbesan," Temileke whispered. "Be cautious. Baale Oşogbesan is a powerful wizard."

"I have hunted many a wizard, my dear," Jalili replied. "I imagine he is no more dangerous than those who have already transitioned from this life at my hand."

"Well, you are *not* to kill *this* one," Temileke hissed. "I simply need you to test his skill, to find out if he is worthy of a spot in the Grand Tournament."

"I do not know why you will not consider my…friend, Jabbar,"

Jalili said. "He is undefeated in countless battles and…"

"He is Urabi," Temileke said, interrupting the eunuch. "Only men of Onile may fight for the hand of our beloved princess."

"Fine," Jalili said, rolling his eyes.

"Besides, I doubt any…*friend* of yours would be interested in marriage to a woman, other than for financial gain." Temileke said.

"Enough chit-chat, Prime Minister," Jalili spat. "Find a safe place from which you can observe. We wouldn't want you to get that pretty face of yours hurt."

*   *   *

Baale Oṣogbesan was making yam pudding.

The old wizard knelt on a small, straw mat, which lay on a patch of worn grass. Before the village chief was a large, black, iron pot, which sat atop a tiny hill of red-hot stones.

Oṣogbesan poured steaming, hot water from a smaller pot into the large pot and then grabbed an iron ladle to stir the mixture of yams, honey and nutmeg.

As Oṣogbesan stirred the yam pudding, Jalili slithered into the shadows of the trees behind his target.

The Baale placed his face close to the pot of yam pudding and inhaled deeply. He closed his eyes and his full lips formed a hint of a smile. The old wizard sighed as the sweet, spicy aroma licked gently at his nostrils.

Jalili crept closer. The assassin leered at the back of Oṣogbesan's neck and the eunuch's muscles—hidden under pudgy rolls of olive-toned flesh—began to tense.

This was his chance. With the wizard out of the way, he was sure he could persuade—or force—Temileke to allow Jabbar into the tournament. He would just make the killing blow look like an accident. Temileke was no warrior. He'd never know.

Jalili bit his flabby bottom lip in anticipation. "One blow," he whispered. "One blow and it's done."

Oṣogbesan dipped the ladle into the large pot and withdrew a mound of sweet yam pudding. He poured the pudding into a wooden bowl that rested beside his left knee.

Jalili strode silently toward the wizard, his large frame moving with surprising speed and agility, until he was within striking distance.

Once again, Oṣogbesan dipped the ladle into the large, iron pot.

Jalili's breath grew shallow as he raised his right palm above his head and slowly torqued his bloated torso to his right. The eunuch's massive arm trembled as he willed pulsing energy into his palm.

Jalili's aṣe—his life-force, which was now guided by the intent to *take* life—screamed to be unleashed. He exhaled as he lurched forward to deliver the powerful blow.

Suddenly, Oṣogbesan turned and extended the bowl of hot yam pudding toward Jalili's chest. "It is always a pleasure when a foreigner pays me a visit."

Jalili was shocked to hear the wizard speak in his native Urabic tongue.

Oṣogbesan smiled as he stared into Jalili's grey eyes, which were open wide with surprise and with fear.

"Here, try some of my yam pudding," Oṣogbesan said, his dark, piercing eyes locking onto Jalili's sickly visage.

The eunuch felt as if he had run into an invisible, impenetrable side of a mountain. All of his killing aṣe dissipated, like the steam that rose from the bowl of yam pudding, swirling into nothingness as it crept toward the eunuch's face.

Jalili shivered and blinked erratically, as if flecks of sand were lodged under his eyelids. He felt naked, vulnerable.

"Sit down," Oṣogbesan calmly commanded.

Jalili looked down at the wizard's mat. Another bowl of yam pudding sat next to it.

Oṣogbesan smiled pleasantly. "Let us eat together, to share brotherhood and to show our mutual good intentions."

Jalili took the bowl of yam pudding into his quivering palms and slowly lowered his massive frame onto the mat until he sat facing

Oṣogbesan. Jalili bowed his head and sobbed. "I never thought my last meal on earth would be a bowl of pounded, sweet yam."

Oṣogbesan blew his cool breath upon a spoonful of hot pudding and replied: "It is better to taste sweetness before coming to a bitter end."

* * *

"Ekaaro, Chief Oṣogbesan!"

Temileke came out of hiding, hoping that his presence would divert Oṣogbesan's attention away from Jalili before the eunuch ate his last spoonful of yam pudding—or anything else, for that matter.

Oṣogbesan peered over his shoulder at Temileke. "So, you have finally decided to show yourself. Come on over and join your friend."

"I assure you, we only meant to test your skill in combat," Temileke said as he walked closer to the wizard and to the sobbing Jalili. "We meant you no permanent or severe harm."

"Why test me then?" Oṣogbesan asked.

"Because I have been sent by the Oba of Oba—the Alaafin, Rogba Adewale—to gather the greatest warriors in Onile for a Grand Tournament. I have heard much about your power and as a student of the arcane, I…"

"Not interested," Oṣogbesan said.

"It is for the hand of the Alaafin's eldest daughter, the lovely Eṣuṣeeke," Temileke said.

"I have *three* wives, all beautiful," Oṣogbesan replied. "Not interested."

"I understand," Temileke sighed. "The Alaafin will be disappointed. He was hoping to give the Aare Ona Kakanfo a challenge."

"Kakanfo Ibikunle?" Oṣogbesan inquired.

"The one and only," Temileke replied.

"Count me in," the wizard said.

"Thank Olodumare!" Temileke said, clapping his hands gleefully. "The Alaafin will be pleased!"

"Take this fat sack of Urabi dog dung with you!" Oṣogbesan spat.

With a wave of the old wizard's hand, Jalili slid off of Oṣogbesan's mat as if a hurricane wind had repelled him.

"Thank you, kind master," Jalili sighed, bowing in reverence and crying with relief.

"Go, before I change my mind," Oṣogbesan said, returning to his bowl of sweet yam pudding.

Jalili pulled his corpulent body to his feet and then backed away from the old wizard, who had defeated him without delivering a strike. Perhaps it was best that Jabbar was not allowed in the tournament. His dear friend was powerful, but Jalili imagined that he had not experienced even a *hint* of what Oṣogbesan could do.

Oṣogbesan turned away from his visitors and turned his thoughts toward the tournament...and revenge for a murdered son.

CHAPTER 12

The nation of Kas was all that Temileke had heard and more. Monolithic pyramids, arranged in a circle with their entrances facing the center, stood in the hub of the capital as eternal testaments to the wisdom and power of Kasthe: inimitable elder sister to Kemet, the jewel of the great Hapi River.

A party of scouts met Temileke mere minutes after he stepped sideways into the capital city of Medewi.

The scouts brought him before the Kentake Amanikhete, the feared woman warrior-king of Kas, who— upon hearing of the Grand Tournament—eagerly summoned the best fighters from within the kingdom and arranged a tournament of her own. It was one of the grueling and brutal tests of skill, strength and intestinal fortitude, designed to find the best possible representative of her nation and of her people in the Grand Tournament of Oyo.

Temileke knelt before the Kentake, who sat upon a throne of ivory at the feet of an immense onyx statue of a pair of wrestlers locked in a tight clinch.

The citizens of Kas had been called to the capital to witness the invitation of their champion to the Grand Tournament.

"You have come to lay eyes upon the greatest warrior the world has ever known, eh, man of Oyo?" The Kentake asked.

"I have come to see your *champion*," Temileke said. "And while I am sure he is formidable never forget, Kentake, the master blacksmith in one town, is the student blacksmith in another."

Kentake Amanikhete's lips curled up into a smile. "The Başorun doubts! A demonstration then?"

Temileke nodded. The Kentake rose from her throne. "The world knows that we—the people of Kas—are a people of war. We are a people who settle our differences with throws, blows, sword and spear. In battle we are *all* outstanding!"

The citizens of Kas roared in agreement, pounding their chests and unleashing a guttural war-cry that gave Temileke chills.

"Most outstanding among we mighty and fierce warriors of Kas is our beloved champion, Kondo," Kentake Amanikhete continued. "Who, with near-inhuman speed and skill, fought and defeated five warriors at once and begged to fight five more in honor of his ten siblings! Kondo, step forward!"

A man with skin like polished, black marble stepped from among the crowd. He was of average height and build, but Temileke had never seen anyone with such extreme definition of sinew. Kondo looked as if every muscle had been painstakingly chiseled by a cosmic sculptor.

The crowd roared once more.

Kondo knelt beside Temileke and kissed the extended hand of his queen.

"Both of you, rise!" The Kentake commanded. Temileke and Kondo sprang to their feet.

"Kondo, a demonstration of your fighting prowess has been requested," Kentake Amanikhete said. "Ready yourself!"

"Hah!" Kondo shouted, beating his chest. The warrior sprinted to the center of his brethren, who had already formed a large circle.

"Summon the Ha-Kri!" The Kentake commanded.

Three young women, dressed only in dark green wrap skirts and armed with small, pointed tree branches, squatted thirty yards from Kondo. The women began to chant in unison, each drawing intricate patterns in the grass-covered soil as they sang:

> *"Makay nabilaa*
> *Makay ki ka nabilaa*
>
> *Foro Bana*
> *Foro Bana*
>
> *Iye laidu mi tanye*
> *Ki bi dem*

Di ne ma
Ningye fro biye
Aiwa makeh ika fro bana

Foro Bana

Iko nyawn fro
Yaye nyawn fro
Iye kuli kro

Foro Bana

Iko malo fro
Soloye malo fro
Iye fon nonon

Foro Bana

Hali fini fro
Finik se
Bonye bele dugu

Foro Bana
Foro Bana

Foro Bina

Foro Bana."

The ground began to tremble. A high-pitched scream erupted from the soil beneath the drawings of the women. The women leapt to their feet, whirled on their heels and sprinted back to the crowd of wide-eyed onlookers.

Suddenly, something tore through the earth, exploding high into the air—something tall and gaunt and of a sickening, aureolin-yellow hue.

Temileke strained his eyes to see the creature clearly, but it seemed to phase in and out of the visible world as it somersaulted through the air.

The creature landed with a thud and Temileke saw it clearly for the first time. The skeletal Ha-Kri seemed to be a creature split down its middle, as it possessed only its left arm, left leg and half its torso and face.

The Ha-Kri's spindly fingers and toes ended in wicked talons of sharpened bone and the white hair on its half-head resembled the quills of the crested porcupine.

"The Ha-Kri is half in and half out of our world," Kentake Amanikhete explained. "Powerful magic keeps the creature from never fully entering our world. For Ha-Kri whole, is unstoppable and possesses an insatiable thirst for human blood."

The monster hopped toward Kondo at an incredible pace, striding three yards with each lurching hop forward. Kondo bent his knees deeply and raised his hands to the height of his chest.

The Ha-Kri leapt toward Kondo, spinning in the air. As the creature's left side turned away from Kondo, the creature vanished.

Suddenly the monster reappeared, its left side once again toward Kondo. The Ha-Kri thrust forward with its leg, driving its heel into Kondo's chest.

The champion of Kas was sent flying backward from the force of the powerful kick. Kondo managed to right himself and landed on his feet, sliding another three yards before coming to a halt.

Kondo charged forward.

The Ha-Kri slashed with its claws.

Kondo, however, was a blur, ducking under the Ha-Kri's attack and popping up behind the creature. Kondo threw a flurry of punches that were barely visible to the eye, each strike tearing into the jaundiced flesh of the Ha-Kri.

Black blood oozed from each wound.

The Ha-Kri unleashed a high-pitched wail and then forcefully snapped its half-head backward. Dart-like quills flew from the monster's scalp.

Kondo moved to evade the quills, side-stepping to his right and then spinning toward his left—the Ha-Kri's non-existent right side.

The Ha-Kri disappeared from Kondo's view again. All but two of the quills sailed harmlessly past Kondo, shattering as they struck the side of one of the pyramids in the distance.

The two quills that met their mark pierced Kondo's chest. Kondo winced from the terrible pain, but continued to press forward.

When the Ha-Kri came into view, Kondo somersaulted forward, whipping his right leg in a circle under him. As Kondo flipped completely over, he brought his right heel down on top of the creature's skull. A sickening, cracking noise followed and the Ha-Kri collapsed.

Once again, the ground rumbled. The earth opened and swallowed its ghastly son, returning it to the dark place from which it came.

Kundo snatched the quills from his chest and then pounded the wounds with his fists. He marched to his queen, and extended the quills toward her.

Kentake Amanikhete took the quills from her champion, and placed them in a small bag that hung from a leather lanyard wrapped around her wrist.

"I will send a retinue to cheer you on to victory and to extol your winning of the Grand Tournament," the Kentake said, giving Kondo a warm and motherly hug.

Temileke had never seen a warrior, even one as womanly as Kentake Amanikhete, be so loving to the warriors under her charge, yet still command such a high level of respect from them. She intrigued him.

"It would please the Başorun of Oyo if Your Highness would be his special guest at the Grand Tournament and sit beside him during the festivities."

"You flatter me, Başorun Temileke," the Kentake replied. "I am quite certain there are many fine women in Oyo —your wives included—who would be overjoyed to sit beside the Prime Minister of such a magnanimous empire as Oyo."

"My wives loathe violence," Temileke said. "And there is no other women in the entire empire that possesses such a combination of beauty, brilliance and boldness as the Kentake Amanikhete!"

"Then, I shall be there to personally raise Kondo's hand in victory," Amanikhete said with a wink.

Temileke smiled. This tournament would be a grand one, indeed.

CHAPTER 13

Temileke used the apere ayorunbo to transport himself to the scorching plains of Kirinyaga, the homeland of the nomadic nation of the Maasai.

Temileke poured water, from a sack made of gazelle hide, into the bowl-shaped apere ayorunbo and then gazed into it. The image of the Maasai village—which had moved thirteen miles south since Temileke's last visit a year ago—appeared in the water.

Temileke placed his left foot into the bowl and warmth came over him. A smell like burnt coffee beans assaulted his nostrils and then the air before him began to shift, to flow, as if it was a vertical river flowing from earth to sky.

An instant later, Temileke stood before the village enkang, the high fence that surrounded the village. The enkang was made from thorny acacia trees, making it well nigh impossible for an enemy or an animal to scale.

Temileke whispered a command and the apere ayorunbo vanished.

A young man, clad in the flowing crimson shuka of the Maasai Moran, opened the gate. "Come in, Elder of Oyo," the warrior said, "the Elders await you."

Temileke stepped through the enkang's gate. The young warrior closed the gate behind Temileke and then led the Baṣorun past the star-shaped inkajijik—the small houses constructed of wood, mud and cow dung in which the Maasai lived—to a small patch of grassland, where elder men and women sat in a circle upon stools padded with cowhide.

Temileke sat upon an empty stool next to the Chief Elder, a man rumored to be well over two hundred years old. The Chief Elder's leathery skin bore the scent of the earth and his thick, calloused hands bore the scars of many battles. Without a word spoken between them, the Chief passed a wooden bowl to Temileke, which the Başorun accepted eagerly.

Temileke brought the bowl to his mouth and drank. The sweet, coppery mixture of milk and cow's blood invigorated him.

"Now, you may speak," the Chief said.

"Thank you, Great Father," Temileke said. "Greetings, Elder Maasai. I come to you today as a representative of the Alaafin of the Oyo Empire."

What is it that your king needs from the Maasai?" The Chief Elder asked.

"He needs only the presence of your greatest warrior, Temileke replied. "For a contest of fighting skill, the likes of which the world has never seen."

"And the prize?" The Chief Elder inquired.

"The hand of the Alaafin's daughter, Eşuşeeke," Temileke answered. "A union between great nations such as ours would bring many blessings."

"Indeed," the Chief nodded. "The greatest among our great warriors is my son, Nangwaya. He has been gone for three days, hunting a lion that has been killing our livestock."

"I pray that your son and the hunting party return victorious and with minimal losses." Temileke said.

"You misunderstand," the Chief Elder replied, shaking his head. "There is no hunting party. Nangwaya is hunting alone. He always hunts alone."

Temileke's eyes widened in amazement. He inhaled deeply to slow his breathing and to regain his composure. Overexcitement in matters of war and the hunt was considered a sign of weakness by the Maasai. "Then, with your permission, I shall remain here to offer praises—and a place in the Grand Tournament—upon his return."

CHAPTER 14

"Nkohbo will be looking forward to his snack when he returns from his swim," Nkonkoni said cheerily as she turned a young goat on the fire.

"Then, perhaps we should begin preparing one for him," Temileke replied.

"The *goat is* my snack!" A bass voice boomed.

Temileke turned toward the voice and came face-to-waist with the famed Zulu warrior, Nkohbo Busisiwe.

Temileke slowly tilted his head backward, taking in the magnificence of the giant. His skin was nearly charcoal black and as smooth as the day he was born. Nkohbo's chest was nearly three times as wide as a normal man's and twice as dense.

The giant's arms had more girth than the average warrior's legs. He stood nearly eight feet tall and it was said that he once brought down a Chitauri—one of the maleficent reptile-men who had waged war with humans for aeons—with a throwing spear from a half-mile away.

"Welcome to Butulozabwei," Nkohbo said with a broad smile. "The most beautiful country in the entire world!"

"Many thanks, Nkohbo," Temileke said, pressing the glowing green stone in his hand to his chest. "Though this is my first visit to the land of the Zulu, it will not be my last!"

What brings you to Butulozabwei?" Nkohbo asked.

Temileke's fetish translated his words into the language of the Zulu: "The Alaafin of the Oyo Empire, Rogba Adewale, is gathering the greatest warriors from across the continent of Onile for a tournament of epic proportions."

"Sounds exciting," Nkohbo said.

"The champion will be given the hand of the Alaafin's beautiful and spirited daughter, Eṣuṣeeke," Temileke replied.

Nkonkoni leapt to her feet and danced around her son excitedly.

"Wait! You mean another woman would be responsible for feeding my son?"

"Why, yes, I suppose so," Temileke snickered.

"Praise Nkulukulu!" Nkonkoni shouted.

"Umama, I did not know you were so eager to be rid of me," Nkohbo said, hanging his massive head.

"I love you dearly, son," Nkonkoni replied. "But, no woman in Butulozabwei will marry you, for fear of you eating the family into poverty, or damaging them in the marriage chamber. This is a chance for me to receive a much deserved respite!"

"Umama has spoken," Nkohbo said, pounding his thick chest with his sledgehammer-like fists. "I will enter—and win

— your tournament!"

"Excellent," the Başorun replied. "I am sure that…"
Suddenly, the largest crocodile Temileke had ever seen in his life burst from behind a bush and charged toward him. Temileke back-pedaled, his eyes wide with fear.

Nkohbo drove the massive heel of his foot down on the crocodile's tail, stopping its charge. The huge reptile hissed and thrashed its head.

"It wanted to make a snack out of you, Prime Minister," Nkohbo snickered. "Now, we will make a snack out of it!"

The giant knelt down and grabbed the crocodile's mouth with his massive hands. Keeping the creature's mouth closed with a tremendous squeeze, Nkohbo forcefully pulled up and back on the crocodile's head. After a few snaps and pops, the reptile lay unmoving.

"Thank you!" Temileke huffed. "I look forward to seeing *you* in the Grand Tournament!"

CHAPTER 15

Akinkugbe and Eṣuṣeeke crept cautiously through the Royal Orchard toward massive Iginla: The Great Tree. Their plain, white, cotton garments glowed a silver-blue in the moonlight.

"It's hot," Akin whispered.

"Then, they are already here. Waiting," Seeke replied.

They both knew well that the uncharacteristic heat in the Royal Orchard indicated the presence of the Oriṣa, or spirits of a more sinister nature. An uncharacteristically cool night would have foretold the presence of the Egungun: the spirits of their ancestors.

This night, the Oriṣa would not grace Akin and Ṣeeke with their presence. Something…else was there, lurking in the shadow of the Great Tree.

Akin held a large, copper plate in both hands. Atop the plate was a steaming pile of viscera, removed from the body of a she-goat the two young warriors had sacrificed, earlier that afternoon, to Orunmila for protection and guidance.

As the couple drew within a yard of Iginla, the gargantuan tree seemed to reach out to them as if it starved for their offering.

Akin knelt at the base of the Great Tree, handing the plate of entrails to Ṣeeke.

Ṣeeke stepped behind Akin and gently pressed the rim of the plate against the back of his neck. The smooth metal felt cool against his sweaty skin.

"Our Mothers, Rulers of the night," Ṣeeke began to chant, closing her eyes:

"Awon Iyawa, I give you respect,
Ancestors, I give you respect,
I give respect to sunrise and to sunset.
Awon Iyawa themselves give me aṣe!

Who can claim to be bigger than the buffalo?
Who can boast being more influential than the Alaafin?
No head-tie can be wider than those used by the elders of the night!
No rope can be as long as the one used by Awon Iyawa,
Our Mothers—the Aje—the witches, whose methodology encompasses and surpasses time!"

A sound, like the cackling of a thousand hens, erupted from the heart of the Great Tree and the base of Iginla convulsed violently.

Şeeke laid the plate at the base of the tree and then knelt beside Akin. Suddenly, the Royal Orchard was engulfed in all-encompassing stark whiteness.

Şeeke and Akin squeezed their eyes shut as the cackling and the whiteness grew more intense. The ground softened and suddenly, Akin felt as if he was kneeling in a warm, syrupy liquid.

The couple pressed the sweaty palms of their hands to their ears as the cackling grew louder and louder.

And then...

Silence.

Akin opened his eyes. Şeeke was already rising to her feet. Akin jumped up to a standing position and then perused his surroundings.

The ground was well kept and the grass was a deep, viridian green. A winding road, constructed of red laterite, led to a network of towering step pyramids, constructed of iron, which crooned an eerie tune as the hot wind battered the ferrous structures.

"Ile Aje," Akin whispered. "The City of Witches!"

* * *

"Are you sure you want to do this?" Şeeke asked. "I appreciate you wanting to give me a special gift. However, I did not think it would entail traveling to the abode of some of the most powerful and most unpredictable creatures in existence!"

"The market-woman, Azen Gasi, assured me that she sent word ahead," Akin replied, "and that we would be safe, as long as we made our purchase from her mother and left immediately afterward."

"I am eager to receive this gift and enjoy it in my chamber tonight!" Şeeke said.

"In other words, you are scared and want to get out of here as quickly as possible!" Akin snickered.

"You are as astute as you are foolhardy, my Lord," Şeeke replied.

A red raven descended onto the winding road before them. The raven stood about half Akin's height. The bird's talons were more like knives than claws. Its blood-red beak ended in a wicked point, and the creature's eyes were as red as its feathers.

Instinctively, Akin's fingers crept toward the ironwood swords which would normally be strapped to his back. But then he recalled that he left them behind because the weapons of man were not permitted in Ile Aje.

The raven shook its head.

Akin's hands returned to his side.

The raven nodded and then pointed a huge wing toward a small step pyramid, which seemed to sit apart from the others.

"That is where we should go?" Akin asked the raven. The raven cawed in affirmation and nodded twice more.

Akin and Şeeke sauntered past the huge bird and walked briskly up the path.

The iron step pyramid was about three stories high. The shiny metal was black, with an orange undertone. Şeeke sniffed the air. The familiar, nutty scent told her that the building's shine and orange tint was attained through the generous use of palm oil, the favorite food of Awon Iyawa.

The half-moon shaped door flew open.

Akin and Şeeke exchanged a quick glance and then Akin entered the pyramid, with Şeeke following closely behind him. The interior of the pyramid was surprisingly well lit and smelled pleasantly of fresh watermelon.

A petite, elderly woman limped from another room into view.

The old woman wore a scarlet wrap skirt and a matching buba. Atop her head was the largest gele Ṣeeke had ever seen. The intricately folded and tied scarlet head-wrap seemed to engulf the tiny woman's skull.

Unraveled, Akin thought, *that thing probably stretches across Onile.*

"You have come for Igi Aiku," the old woman said.

"Yes, umm…Good Mother," Akin answered.

The old woman glared at Akin. "You hesitate to call me good. Why?"

"N-no offense, Good Mother," Akin replied. "I see that your color is red and I thought—"

"You thought that goodness is reserved for only my sisters of the White Order." The old woman said, interrupting him.

"Yes, Iyami," Akin said.

"You humans are so confused," the old witch chuckled. "Where would you be without that old flirt, Orunmila to guide you?"

"Without the guidance of Ifa, our ignorance would be ignorant, Iyami," Akin replied.

"Just so you know, our colors have nothing to do with good or evil," the old woman said. "The Awon Iyawa are neither good, nor evil, yet we are both. We are everything…and nothing."

"Thank you, for the lesson, Iyami," Akin said.

"I am not done, boy!" The elder witch snapped.

Akin swallowed hard and wiped the sweat from his bowed head. "Apologies, My Mother."

A smile spread over the old woman's face. "So respectful. I like you, boy!"

"Mo dupe, Iyami!" Akin replied.

"I have not decided about the Princess yet!" The old woman said, leering at Ṣeeke. "My name is Yaba Yinka, by the way. But if you call me by name, I will have to kill you, okay?"

"Beni, Iyami," Akin and Ṣeeke said in unison.

"Now, to continue your lesson," Yaba Yinka began. "The color black is the color of perfection, vitality and infinite depth. My sisters who wear white wear the colors of spiritual transcendence and we, of the Red Order, wear the color of aṣe, the power of Creation."

Şeeke and Akin remained silent.

"I am done," Yaba Yinka said. "You can thank me for the lesson now."

"A dupe, Iyawa!" Akin and Şeeke said together. "We thank you, Our Mother!"

"Ko tope!" Yaba Yinka replied. "Wait here!" The old witch commanded.

Yaba Yinka limped out of the room. A moment later, she returned carrying a tiny iroko tree, which rested in a red, clay pot. The tree was about the size of a man's torso. Its thick, bushy, dark green leaves seemed to mimic the immense gele resting upon Yaba Yinka's head.

"Here is Igi Aiku," Yaba Yinka said, "the Forever Tree. It is immortal, and wards off any harmful spirits from whatever home it is put in."

Yaba Yinka handed the tree to Şeeke. The Princess admired the tree as you brought it close to her face. "Beautiful, and it smells divine!"

"And it is yours for only five hundred thousand cowries!" Yaba Yinka said, smiling.

"Five hundred thousand?!" Akin gasped. "Azen Gasi quoted me a price of two hundred thousand, Iyami."

"That was the price *yesterday*," Yaba Yinka said. "Today is another day."

"I cannot afford that much, Iyami," Akin sighed.

"Oh, dear, what are you going to do?" Yaba Yinka asked.

"There is nothing I *can* do, Iyami," Akin replied.

"It is alright, my Lord. You *wanted* to give me this gift," Şeeke said, kissing Akin on the cheek. "Your heart was in it. That is all that matters to me!"

"Oh, how sweet," Yaba Yinka said, folding her hands under her chin. "I like you too, now, Princess."

"Mo dupe, Iyami," Şeeke said.

"I tell you what, boy," the old witch began. "Let's make a trade. I will *give* you the Igi Aiku...*if* you take me to
    earth with you."

"Take you to earth?" Akin inquired. "Surely you possess the power to travel to Aiye just as your daughter does."

"Azen Gasi has a human father," Yaba Yinka replied. "We full-blooded Awon Iyawa are banned by Olodumare from setting foot on Aiye."

"Then, how can *I* possibly help you, Iyami?" Akin asked.

"I cannot set *foot* on Aiye, but should I hitch a ride in your stomach, it will be *your* feet touching down on Aiye, not mine!"

Akin scratched his head as he contemplated Yaba Yinka's offer. "Hitch. A ride. In my…stomach?"

"It is not as painful as it sounds, my dear boy," the old witch replied. "You will hardly even know I'm there. Just a little pinch here and there."

"Well…okay," Akin said. "I…"

"Good! It is done!" Yaba Yinka said.

The witch vanished.

A moment later, Akin felt a stabbing pain in his gut.

"Let's get going," a muffled voice shouted through the muscular walls of his belly. "Aiye awaits!"

CHAPTER 16

Akin and Ṣeeke returned to earth in a flash of light. It was still dark in the Royal Orchard.

"We are here, Good Mother," Akin said, grasping at his aching belly. "You may come out now."

"I told you, I cannot set foot on Aiye," Yaba Yinka replied.

"You can fly, can't you?" Ṣeeke asked.

"Of course," Yaba Yinka answered. "This is much more relaxing, though."

"Please, come out, Iyami," Akin sighed. "Your inhabiting my belly hurts!"

"No, I think I will stay a while," Yabba Yinka replied. "Perhaps an eternity."

Akin faked a laugh. "Your wit is quick and your comedic timing is unmatched, Iyami!"

Ṣeeke joined in with Akin's laughter. "You are too funny, Iyami. When you come out, I am going to give you the biggest hug!"

"Your grandchildren will be old before I receive that hug, child!" Yaba Yinka said. "I am not coming out!"

"You will starve if you stay in there, Iyami," Akin said.

"I will eat what *you* eat," Yaba Yinka replied.

"Then I won't eat!" Akin said defiantly. "You will starve to death."

"Then, I will make a meal of your intestines and your liver," Yaba Yinka replied. Akin threw up his hands in frustration and exasperation.

Ṣecke placed her hands on Akin's broad chest. "Calm down, my Lord. We will take care of this."

"How?" Akin sighed.

"Sit…I will go find a solution," Ṣeeke replied. "Trust me, my Lord; you are going to be fine soon!"

Akin sat down at the base of Iginla. He drew his knees to his chest and rested his forehead on his knees. "I *do* trust you. Go!"

Şeeke picked up the tiny Forever Tree and tucked it under her arm; then she kissed Akin on the forehead, turned and sprinted out of the Royal Orchard.

The Princess continued to run, concealing herself in shadow, lest the patrolling guards see her and report to her father that she was out and about at strange hours of the night.   She had to keep her friendship with the Aare Ona Kakanfo a secret until after the Grand Tournament, because people would think the competition was fixed in The
Kakanfo's favor.

The Princess arrived at an elegant house, painted forest green, with brown trimming around the windows. The door was made of mahogany, on the face of which was carved a scene of a babalawo divining for a couple in a forest clearing. A huge tree loomed in the background. On the branches of the tree sat sixteen tiny birds.

Şeeke curled her fingers into a fist and raised her arm in preparation to knock on the door. But before she could, the door slid open a crack and a voice whispered. "Come in, Princess!"

Şeeke slipped through the doorway into darkness. Suddenly, the room was bathed in soft lantern light. Şeeke looked around, taking in her surroundings. The room was large and empty, except for the plush, cotton pillows—filled with guinea fowl feathers—that were strewn about the room...and Baba Fafore, who sat upon his mat with his back resting against the far wall. Sitting before him were his divining cloth and his opele.

"You are wise, Baba. You knew that I had come for divination," Şeeke said.

"No, I am old," Baba Fafore replied. "So, I knew you had not come for an intimate tryst. What other need would you have of me?"

Şeeke laughed. "Mo dupe for seeing me at this late
hour, Baba."

"Ko tope, Your Majesty," Baba Fafore said. "Now, sit and let us begin." Şeeke sat across from Baba Fafore, resting her weary bottom on a soft pillow.

Baba Fafore picked up the opele and pressed the divining chain to Ṣeeke forehead. He then pressed it to her chest. The old high priest brought the divining chain close to his face and blew a quick breath on each seed. He made a brief, silent prayer and tossed the chain onto the mat...studying the configuration of the seeds, picked up the chain and threw it twice more in the same manner.

He then stared into Ṣeeke's eyes, accessing her spirit and her soul. After a brief silence, Baba Fafore spoke. "Ifa says you have come to inquire about someone else. Someone you love."

"Yes, Baba," Ṣeeke replied. "But I—"

"You need to keep your feelings a secret," Baba Fafore said, interrupting her. Ṣeeke nodded.

"I know. Ifa sees all, child," Baba Fafore said. "The Odu that has fallen is Osa Meji. Your friend has had a run in with the witches."

"Yes, Baba," Ṣeeke replied. A powerful witch named…"

"Do *not* speak her name, Ṣeeke!" Baba Fafore warned.

"She will kill you if you do! Ifa says her name is Yaba Yinka."

"Baba!" Ṣeeke shouted, as she sat bolt upright in shock.

"The Mothers can do no harm to a representative of Orunmila, Princess," Baba Fafore said. "Lest they incite the wrath of their mistress, Odu—wife of Orunmila—who promised him that as long as he and his representatives continued to do good in the world, none of her children would harm them."

"The witch has taken up residence in my…friend's belly and refuses to leave, Baba," Ṣeeke said. "She has threatened to eat his innards and is causing him great pain."

Baba Fafore closed his eyes and began to chant:

"It is as heavy as lead
Even with the rainstorm, the witches are never disturbed
Divined for Orunmila,
Who was the only Oriṣa who made a pact with the witches
At the beginning of time,
When the witches were coming to earth from the spirit
world.
Orunmila asked them, 'Where are you going?'

They told him that they were going to earth
Orunmila asked, 'What is your mission there?'
The witches answered that their mission was to wreck
havoc
And to compound problems for those who have   problems.
Orunmila told them to go back to the spirit world.
They appealed to Orunmila to not send them back.
Orunmila told them that his children are many on
earth.
The witches suggested a covenant with Orunmila
Orunmila told them that he did not know
What the instruments of the oath were.
The witches told Orunmila to give akara—fried bean
balls.
That day, they swore an oath before Orunmila
And promised that whenever they came across
Someone who is immunized with akara,
They would never bother such a person.
Orunmila said, 'I have heard your promise and it is
noted.
But what if one of you refuses or breaks this oath?'
They replied, 'Should any witch not abide by this oath,
A slippery substance will make said witch
Slip to the sphere of no return.'"

Baba Fafore opened his eyes. "You must cook sixteen akara and sit them before your friend. This will draw Yaba Yinka out."

Ṣeeke rose from her seat. "Mo dupe, Baba! I will have the royal chef whip up a batch immediately!"

"No," Baba Fafore said, waving a crooked finger. "*You* must cook the bean balls. No one else."

"But, Baba, I have never cooked a day in my life!" Ṣeeke said.

"You will be a wife soon. You must learn to cook," Baba Fafore said. "And there is no time like the present."

Ṣeeke nodded. "Mo dupe, Baba. I will send payment to you

for the divination."

"Consider it a wedding gift," Baba Şeeke said. "And Şeeke, the friend you help is more…and less…than you think he is."

Şeeke squinted her eyes and tilted her head sideways. "More *and* less…? Would you care to explain, Baba?"

"No," Baba Fafore replied.

Al…right, then," Şeeke said. "I will leave you now, Baba."

"Odabo," Baba Fafore said.

"Odabo," Şeeke said in return. She walked backward to the door, turned and headed back out into the night.

CHAPTER 17

Ikeade strolled into the kitchen just before dawn. Her lean frame was covered in a form-fitting, blue dress and her hair was covered in a white gele.

"What are you fixing for breakfast this morning, Royal Chef?"

Ikeade turned toward the voice. "Princess Eṣuṣeeke, you startled me!"

"Ekaaro, Ikeade," Ṣeeke said. "How are you?"

"Ekaaro," Ṣeeke replied. "I am fine, Your Majesty. How are you?"

"I am fine," Ṣeeke said.

"Forgive me," Ikeade said, frowning. "But I have never seen you in my kitchen before. To what do I owe this visit?"

"I…I need your help," Ṣeeke said.

"*My* help?" Ikeade said, surprised. "How can I assist you? I could not fight my way out of an open calabash, so…"

"Oh, no, I do not need you to help me fight anyone," Eṣuṣeeke snickered. "I need you to teach me how to cook akara."

"Why do you need to learn to cook akara?" Ikeade asked.

"Well, as you know, I am to marry soon," Ṣeeke replied. "I want to be able to cook good meals for my husband. I figured I would start with something simple."

"Akara tastes good, but it is hardly a good meal," Ikeade chuckled. "I will teach you…under one condition…"

"Name your condition and I will meet it!" Ṣeeke said confidently.

Ikeade hung her head. A blanket of sadness spread across her face. "Do you know of the Kpelekpe?"

"The shape-shifting hyena-men?" Ṣeeke said. "Of course."

"Ten years ago, Hagagah—the Lord of the Kpelekpe— took my only son from me," Ikeade sighed. "Hagagah called to my baby with that chilling laugh one night, and my son could not resist. He was not yet able to walk, so he crawled out the door while my husband and I slept and went to the hyena-man."

A tear rolled down Ikeade's cheek. "The next morning, our son's bones and hair were found; and Hagagah—who had been posing as a hunter named Olode—was also gone. Divination confirmed that Olode was, in actuality, Hagagah."

"I am so sorry for your loss, Ikeade," Ṣeeke said. "How can I be of assistance?"

"Hagagah has returned to Oyo," Ikeade said. "He lives in the forests just outside the walls surrounding Metropolitan Oyo. In his old age, the creature does not bother to take human form any longer—or perhaps he cannot—either way, he is just as dangerous."

"A few days ago, he attacked a hunting party. Only one survived and he will probably die soon. The Alaafin has put off any search for the monster until after the tournament. I fear Hagagah will soon disappear again."

"And what do you want *me* to do?" Ṣeeke asked.

"I know you are well-trained in the combat arts," Ikeade replied. "Kill Hagagah and bring his body to me, so I can prepare a stew out of him, and I will teach you to make akara."

"If the beast killed an entire hunting party, what chance do *I* have?" asked Ṣeeke.

"If you want to learn to cook akara from *me* you will find a way." Ikeade replied.

"Okay, I will bring you Hagagah's corpse," Ṣeeke said. "But these had better be the best akara to ever touch a person's lips or you will join the hyena-man in the pot!"

"It is a deal, Your Majesty," Ikeade said, bowing her head.

*   *   *

Ṣeeke sat under a tree in the dense forest finishing off a ripe, juicy mango. Her eyes were closed as she ate. Ṣeeke licked her fingers and, with her eyes still pressed tightly shut, tossed the mango seed away with the flick of her wrist.

I pray this works, thought Ṣeeke, as she reached, with blind hands, into the basket beside her to retrieve another mango.

After a few bites of the sweet fruit, Ṣeeke heard a rustling of leaves, followed by what was, unmistakably, heavy breathing and a rank smell of musk.

"Is it *good?"* A raspy voice asked.

"Who is there?" Ṣeeke gasped. Her eyes remained closed.

"A *friend,*" the voice said. "My name is Hagagah. And you are?"

"I am Abiola Oṣunkemi," Eṣuṣeeke lied. "And yes, the mango is delicious."

"What are you doing in the forest all alone, child?" Hagagah asked. Ṣeeke could almost hear the sly smile spread across the monster's face. "Besides, of course, eating delicious mango?"

"I am admiring the view of Heaven," Ṣeeke replied. "It is more beautiful than I ever imagined!"

"Admiring the view…are you not blind, child?" Hagagah inquired.

"No," Ṣeeke answered. "I have merely sewn my eyelids shut, as my Egungun instructed me."

Ṣeeke felt Hagagah's hot breath against her face. The smell of raw meat and curdled milk assaulted her, and she had to fight back the urge to vomit.

"I see no thread in your eyelids, child," Hagagah said. "Do you mock me, little one?"

"I do not know you, to mock you, sir," Ṣeeke said. "The thread I used was made from spider's silk, so it is very thin. Look in my basket and you will see it."

Ṣeeke heard a rustling through her basket. A moment later, she felt the spool of thread drop into her lap.

"Why don't you do old Hagagah a favor and help me get a peek into Heaven," the were-hyena said.

"Oh, no, I could never do that," Ṣeeke said. "With my eyes sewn together by the spider's silk, I can not only *see* into Orun, I can touch and be touched. I can feel the soft sand beneath my feet and drink of the heavenly waters."

"Please, child," Hagagah crooned. "Indulge an old man!"

"Oh, alright," Ṣeeke replied. "But if Olodumare asks how you got there, do not mention *my* name."

"You have my word—my lips shall remain as sealed as my eyelids," Hagagah said.

A massive hand guided Ṣeeke's arm upward. She felt the pinch of the creature's claws on her forearms. With needle and thread in her fingers, Ṣeeke began to sew.

Once her work was done on one eye, Hagagah guided Ṣeeke to the other. The young woman sewed, careful to keep the stitches close together and very tight.

Ṣeeke slowly opened her eyes. She jumped to her feet when she saw the huge creature before her. Its head was large, with a thick jaw and its stout, hyena's face, covered in short, smooth, tan fur. Hagagah's back was hunched as it sat on its hind legs, the creature's thick, furry tail slithering beneath its buttocks.

The Kpelekpe was covered too, in matted, spotted fur of a hue slightly darker than its face. Its short, thick, hind-legs were like those of a common, spotted hyena. The creature's long, powerful, fore-legs were covered in short fur, but were more like the arms of a great ape and ended in calloused, clawed, human hands.

"Will I see Heaven soon?" Hagagah asked.

"Oh, yes," Ṣeeke replied, slowly drawing a keen hunting knife from within the folds of her dress. "Very soon, indeed!"

Ṣeeke lunged forward, driving the blade, up to the hilt, into Hagagah's throat. The were-hyena bellowed and swung its paws wildly, just missing Ṣeeke's belly.

Ṣeeke slashed inward, cutting through Hagagah's esophagus. The blade tore through the flesh of the creature's neck. Blood sprayed from the monster's severed carotid arteries and gushed from its jugular vein, painting the grass shades of crimson and bright red.

Hagagah convulsed violently for a few moments and then lay,

unmoving, in a puddle of its own gore.

Ṣeeke knelt beside Hagagah's corpse and quickly wrapped spider's silk around its sticky neck. Ṣhe pulled and the massive Kpelekpe slid easily across the grass. Ṣeeke felt as if she was pulling a half-full water-skin instead of a creature the size of a horse.

The magical spider's silk the Baṣorun, Temileke, had given her on her fifteenth birthday had finally been of some use.

Ṣeeke turned her back to the were-hyena and jogged forward, dragging the creature's corpse behind her.

CHAPTER 18

Akin heard a rustling in the distance. He slowly raised his head from his knees, ignoring the grating pain in his gut.

Someone was sprinting toward him—a woman, tall…athletic. A calabash was held out in front of her. The noonday sun was at the woman's back, which gave her a golden glow.

"Yeye Oṣun?" Akin asked. *Has the Oriṣa Oṣun, Matron of the Red Order of witches, come to save me from one of her sisters?* he wondered.

As the woman drew near, Akin saw that it was not Oṣun, but her and Baba Eṣu's spiritual daughter, Ṣeeke. He forced a smile. "Ekaale!"

"Good afternoon to you, too, my Lord," Ṣeeke replied. "I have a gift for you that will solve your…issue."

"A gift I am most eager to receive," Akin said.

Ṣeeke sat beside Akin and placed the calabash at his feet. She removed the white cloth covering it and a delicious smell enveloped his face.

"Akara!" A muffled voice shouted from within Akin's bowels.

Akin spasmed violently and retched.

Ṣeeke sprang up onto her heels in a squatting position and placed her hands upon Akin's shoulders. "My Lord, what is wrong?"

Akin tried to speak but the words could not escape his constricted throat. He retched again…and again.

Suddenly, a small, gelatinous orb— vermilion in hue —flew from Akin's open mouth.

The orb began to pulsate. Akin jumped to his feet and backed away from it. Ṣeeke followed suit.

The orb opened and stretched and twisted and coiled, spiraling in upon itself...shaping, un-shaping...until before them sat Yaba Yinka,

Lord and Lady of the Red Order of Awon Iyawa.

Akin touched his belly. The pain in it was gone.

Yaba Yinka snatched a fistful of akara from the calabash and tossed them into her gaping mouth.

As the witch happily devoured the spicy-sweet, fried bean balls Akin and Ṣeeke crept away from her. When they were a good distance from the witch, they broke into a full run, not stopping until they were well away from the Royal Orchard.

Ṣeeke grabbed Akin's arm. He turned to face her. The princess' eyes were slits and her lips were curled into a scowl. "My Lord, while I appreciate you going to extremes to give

me a gift, do not *ever* put yourself in danger like that again!" Ṣeeke spat. "You could have died! *I* could have died! There is nothing, or no one that…"

"I love you, Ṣeeke," Akin said, interrupting her.

Ṣeeke's expression softened. She looked up into Akin's eyes as she inched closer to him. "I love you too."

Akin pulled Ṣeeke to him and held her in his muscular arms. "The tournament is a fortnight away," Ṣeeke said, resting her head upon Akin's sinewy chest.

"I know! We have waited two seasons for this. I am excited!" Akin replied.

"You *have* to win!" Ṣeeke cried.

"Don't worry, my love," Akin said, gently massaging Ṣeeke's temples with his thumbs. "I *will*."

"Promise me!" Ṣeeke replied.

"I promise you that *nothing* and no *one* will stop me from winning your hand," Akin said.

"Good," Ṣeeke replied, gazing lovingly into Akin's eyes. "Because you have already won my *heart*."

CHAPTER 19

The elders among the townspeople had directed Temileke to the deep forest, where Kongo legend told of Runihara: great destroyer of armies, terror of the forest, slayer of monsters, ghosts and even demigods.

Temileke dozed in his litter, shut off—by a door and four windows made of green glass beads—from the squad of mercenaries he hired to find Runihara and test the legend's skill.

A piercing scream jolted the Başorun out of his slumber. The scream was followed by another and another. A massive shadow slithered across the litter's doorway. The mercenaries had obviously found Runihara and were regretting their discovery.

The silence, after the screams, fell over the litter like a moist blanket.

Temileke poked his head out of the door of his litter and quickly perused his surroundings. All twenty of the mercenaries were dead; their bodies in jagged pieces, as if torn apart by some rabid beast.

Temileke darted his head back into the litter and whispered a command.

The iron handles of the litter bent and twisted until they formed two ostrich-like legs. The animated litter lurched forward, trotting at first and then building to a sprint, taking long strides through the dense forest.

Temileke breathed a sigh of relief as the litter carried him swiftly away from the grisly scene of carnage.

Suddenly, a dark figure burst through the door of the litter and landed, with a resounding thud, on the floor of the litter, in front of Temileke.

The Başorun sprang into a kneeling position on the couch within the litter. His heart pounded erratically and a rivulet of perspiration ran down his forehead and into his eyes, stinging them.

Standing before Temileke was the dreaded Runihara…all four feet, six inches of him.

"I hear you are looking for me," Runihara hissed.

"Y-yes," Temileke replied. "My emperor is hosting a tournament of the best fighters in Onile."

"And the prize?" Runihara asked.

"Marriage to the Alaafin's daughter," Temileke answered.

"Is she pretty?" Runihara asked.

"Very," Temileke replied.

"Is she tasty?" Runihara inquired.

"Tasty? I…I don't know", Temileke said, shaking his head.

"Who *does* know?" Runihara spat, baring his shark-like teeth.

Temileke stared into Runihara's mouth. The stout, little man's teeth appeared to be razor-sharp and forged from iron. Spots of rust decorated the teeth. A chill came over Temileke and he quickly turned his attention to the scenery outside of the windows of his litter.

"No one, as far as I know," Temileke replied. "The Princess has never been the victim of cannibals *and* she is a virgin, so…"

"A virgin?" Runihara shouted, licking his lips. Mmm…then she *is* tasty! I accept your invitation!"

CHAPTER 20

A volley of Ẹṣọ arrows fell, like iron-tipped raindrops, upon the heads of the Urabi soldiers who, earlier that day, had launched an attack on the Northern Border of the Oyo Empire.

Those not quick enough, or too injured to raise their shields, fell as the keen arrows sliced through the copper helmets of the Urabi and impaled their skulls.

The Urabi countered with their munujuniq—*The stone slinger*—a massive, wheeled monstrosity that hurled half-ton stones onto the battlefield from the rear of the Urabi forces.

A stone whistled across the humid, early morning sky as it sped toward the forces of Oyo. Scores of Oyo warriors scattered to avoid the falling stone cloud. Many evaded it. Many did not.

An entire squad of Oyo spearmen disappeared beneath the great stone, which landed on the soil with a tremendous thud. The ground sank beneath the stone's weight and those within two yards of the tremor caused by the stone were sent sailing through the air.

The forces of Oyo quickly regrouped and charged forward, determined to get to the Urabi's rear line before they could load another stone.

The Aare Ona Kakanfo looked out on the blood-soaked land beneath him.

Wave after wave of Urabi soldiers fell under Oyo sword, arrow and spear.

The mighty Ẹṣọ led the warriors of Oyo in the drive against the Urabi hordes, and they quickly encroached upon the Urabi rear line.

Suddenly a path of ebony, indigo and sand began to form at the rear of the battlefield. The Kakanfo raised his spyglass to his eye and focused on the growing path. A Captain of the Urabi Army was carving a swath of destruction through the forces of Oyo.

The large Urabi rode upon a muscular, armored war-camel, the common steed of the Urabi, his scimitar flashing from side-to-side. As the weapon struck flesh, sand—not blood—poured from the wounds it inflicted.

"Dark Urabi magic," the Kakanfo said, slipping his spyglass into a pocket on his saddle.

The War Chief of War Chiefs snapped his warhorse's reins. The horse exploded forward and the Kakanfo drew the Invincible Staff as he charged down the hill.

Kakanfo Ibikunle raced toward the rear line, his horse leaping over Oyo and Urabi corpses and dodging the slash of Urabi cutlasses.

The Aare Ona Kakanfo hurled the Invincible Staff at the chest of the Urabi Captain.

The Invincible Staff emitted a low hum and a steadily intensifying glow as it sped toward its target.

The Staff struck, but seemed to do no damage as it bounced off the Urabi Captain's burnished, bronze chest-plate. The Invincible Staff flew back into the Aare Ona Kakanfo's awaiting hand.

Suddenly, the Urabi Captain's chest-plate began to hum—like a tuning fork—in synchrony with the hum of the Invincible Staff. The sound, soft at first, grew louder...and louder...and...*louder*.

Torrents of blood erupted from the Urabi Captain's every orifice.

The same fate was shared by the Captain's hump-backed steed. The camel collapsed onto its belly, throwing its rider. The poor beast convulsed violently as blood continued to flow.

The Urabi Captain tumbled across the grassy plain, leaving a trail of gore behind him.

The dying man rolled to a stop—his once tawny skin now a sickly bluish-grey. The Urabi Captain's limbs flopped wildly for a moment and then he lay still.

The humming of the Invincible Staff ceased.

The Aare Ona Kakanfo's Herald, Abe, rode up on his light warhorse. The beautiful, chestnut-brown horse sported less armor than the steeds belonging to the other Eṣo, for it was bred more for speed than for power.

"You sent for me, my Lord?" Abe shouted over the battle cries, clashes of metal and screams of agony.

"Yes," the Kakanfo replied. "Return to Metropolitan Oyo. Arrange a meeting with the Alaafin and request that he postpone the Grand Tournament. The Hausa have converted to the religion of the Urabi and now swell the forces of these sand-dwelling dogs! I must remain here to keep the enemy from crossing our borders!"

"Yes, my Lord!" Abe said.

"Be *swift*, Abe!" The Aare Ona Kakanfo commanded.

"Yes, my Lord!"

Abe yanked his horse's reins and the horse sped off, kicking up tiny hills of blood-soaked earth with each swift step.

CHAPTER 21

The Oja-oba was busier than usual, with visitors from across Onile, and beyond, descending upon Oyo to witness what promised to be the greatest contest of martial skill in the history of man.

Spectators from each of the seven continents: Onile, Sighashri, Hoostheim, Inkmehez Celtshire, Matongpa, and Apanakoti, were in attendance.

All were at the market—marveling at the wares and spending large sums of money.

Among the patrons was the wizard, Chief Oṣogbesan.

A hooded, dark brown frock concealed the wizard's face. The worn frock also hid the forest green buba and ṣokoto he wore underneath it. The only indication that Oṣogbesan was not a pauper was his shoes, also forest green, which were crafted from Chitauri hide. The shoes were magic fetishes, granting Oṣogbesan amazing speed and reptilian agility, despite his venerable age.

The old wizard strolled westward, to the edge of the marketplace, where the arena—named Ile Ogun, or *House of the Orișa Ogun*—sat in all its glory.

Ile Ogun—like the Orișa after whom it was named— descended deep into the bowels of the earth. Constructed entirely of earth and stone, the vast arena resembled a crater.

A ramp spiraled down, offering access to the first and second balconies and to the main floor. The Royal Terrace was carved into the West wall and was accessible only through a secret tunnel concealed within the sub-basement of the palace.

The Warriors' Pen was located on the main floor and accessible by a second ramp, which zigzagged its way to the floor of the arena.

The Alaafin had paid a large sum—in cowries, honey and palm wine—to hire the fierce Mino, the famed "Amazons" of the Kingdom of Dahomey. The Mino were guards without equal, yet also very pleasing to the eye in their gilt skirts, greaves, breastplates, bracelets, armlets and helmets.

The Mino patrolled the surface around the arena and within Ile Ogun's depths, controlling access and maintaining peace and order.

Oṣogbesan stared down into the chasm that was Ile Ogun. In less than a fortnight, he would meet the Aare Ona Kakanfo in the Circle of Sand. In less than a fortnight, he would avenge his son's murder at the hands of the Kakanfo, or he would perish in the attempt.

CHAPTER 22

The long hallway, within the opulent palace of Shekhem Fet Bin Fet, seemed to go on forever as Jalili strutted its length.

The sound of metal crashing against metal echoed throughout the east wing of the palace.

Jalili recognized the dissonant sound—gladiators, practicing with blunt swords, under the watchful and cruel eye of Jabbar, "the Demon."

Jabbar had been hired to whip the gladiators of Kamet into shape, as the Shekhem loved to gamble on fights, but hated to lose.

Jabbar, the Demon's reputation as a soldier, strategist and trainer of killers was known from throughout the continent of Sighashri to the southern borders of Onile.

Jabbar's albescent face lit up as Jalili entered the room. He desired to embrace his dearest of friends in their special and intimate way, but such affection between men was unheard of in Kamet—or, in truth, on the entire continent of Onile.

The former Commander of the armed forces of Urabin had retired and moved with Jalili from their homeland, where their… friendship was punishable by death, in hopes of amassing enough wealth to relocate to the continent of Celtshire, where the special bond he shared with Jalili was relatively commonplace.

Jabbar was well on his way. Marriage to the daughter of the Alaafin of the Oyo Empire would gain him enough wealth to live out his days comfortably in the rolling meadows of Longshanks, the wealthiest nation on the continent of Celtshire.

"Us-sulum Ulokam," Jabbar greeted Jalili in the Urabic tongue.

"Wulokam sulum," Jalili replied.

"What good news do you bring me?" Jabbar asked. His voice was gravelly, harsh, as if he had swallowed a fistful of sand.

"I regret that I am the bearer of no good news this day," Jalili replied.

"What is wrong?" Jabbar inquired.

"The Başorun of Oyo—the representative of the Alaafin—has denied you entry into the Grand Tournament."

Jabbar's leathery, alabaster face twisted into a scowl. He grabbed Jalili's meaty left wrist and pulled him away from the gladiators.

"Water break!" The Demon shouted over his shoulder.

The gladiators ceased sparring and lined up at the water barrels to pour themselves a cup and to chat about women and wine and past victories. More than a few times, the Grand Tournament of Oyo came up and many whispered their desire to fight in such a competition.

Gladiators were slaves, however, and the Grand Tournament would be fought by free men—chiefs, warlords and maybe even a king was the rumor.

Jabbar's grip on Jalili's arm tightened as they moved from earshot of the gladiators.

"*Ow!*" Jalili groaned. "You're hurting me!"

"You *promised* me you would get me into that tournament!" Jabbar hissed.

"I tried!" Jalili cried. "But, Urabin and the Oyo Empire *are* at war. So—not surprisingly—there is tension between the Urabi and the Oyo right now! Furthermore, the Başorun, Temileke, made it quite clear that only *dark-skinned* inhabitants of Onile are welcome to compete."

"Those tar-hued infidels deny *me*?" Jabbar spat, slapping his pale chest. "Well, I will make them see the error of their ways. Pack our things, Jalili! We leave for Quraish at nightfall!"

Jalili nodded and turned to leave. "I will see you later, Jabbar. Why not kill one of the gladiators? It will brighten your mood."

Jabbar smiled. "I will kill three. Three will make me happy!"

"Have at it then," Jalili said, as he sashayed off.

Jabbar whirled around to face the gladiators. He marched into the middle of the hardened men and assumed a wide fighting stance.

The Demon held no weapons. "The first man to sever one of my limbs wins his freedom!"

Without a second thought, a short, lean man with yellowish-brown skin leaped toward Jabbar. The daggers that protruded from his boots flashed by Jabbar's face as both legs whipped around in a flashy aerial kick.

Jabbar took a step back. "Are you trying to scare me, little bird?"

The small man's face remained stoic. He skipped forward and then launched another kick, thrusting the toes of his right foot—and the point of the boot-dagger—at Jabbar's belly.

Jabbar caught the man's leg with his left hand. "Got you, little bird!"

The gladiator leap off of his left leg and then twisted to his right. He whipped his left leg in a wide arc across Jabbar's right side.

Jabbar winced in pain as the gladiator's boot-dagger sliced through the muscles, tendons and bone of his right forearm. However, he did not loosen his grip on the gladiator's leg with his left hand.

Jabbar looked down at his arm. It was hanging by a thick strip of flesh. Jabbar smiled. "Almost…but the arm is not severed. No freedom for you, little bird!"

Jabbar squeezed with all his might. His left hand closed around the gladiator's ankle tighter and tighter. The gladiator screamed as the small bones in his ankle were pulverized to dust. The Demon lifted the gladiator by his ankle, hoisting him high into the air.

Jabbar then slammed the man to the floor with such force, the marble floor cracked and a spider-web of stress lines crept outward from under the gladiator's shattered spine.

The gladiator's eyes rolled back in his head and his body went limp.

Jabbar grabbed his right wrist with his left hand and pressed the hanging bottom of his forearm to the top. The flesh began to twitch and then to stitch itself back together. After a few moments, Jabbar's right arm was functional again and only a deep scar near his elbow indicated that it was ever injured at all.

I am feeling better, already, Jabbar thought. "Well, come on then! Wenches and ale to anyone who survives!"

As the gladiators charged forward, Jabbar smiled. "Aah, nothing like a bit of carnage to lift the spirits!"

CHAPTER 23

Abe brought his horse to a stop at a modest house in the Ajaland layer of the empire. The cool, evening air carried the pleasant scent of watermelon, green pepper and recent rain.

"Ekurole," Abe said in greeting. "Good evening! Is anyone home?"

The door of the house creaked open. A man of medium complexion and medium build stepped outside. Holding the man's hand and walking closely behind him, was a beautiful, mahogany-toned woman whose belly was heavy with child.

"Greetings, sir!" the man said.

"Greetings! How may we assist you?" the woman chimed in.

Abe leapt down from his horse. He extended his right hand toward the man. "Greetings, family! I am Abe, Herald of our great Aare Ona Kakanfo!"

The man shook Abe's hand and then prostrated in salute. The woman bent her knees deeply in salutation.

"I request accommodations for the night," Abe said with a broad smile.

"You are more than welcome to stay here, my Lord," the man said. "I am Bayo and this is my wife, Toki. Are you headed back to Metropolitan Oyo?"

"Yes, to the palace," Abe replied.

Toki waddled toward the house, gesturing, with a wave of her hand, for the men to follow. "That is about a two days' ride from here. Come inside. I will fix you something to eat."

Abe followed the couple into the great room, where Toki rolled out a slightly worn mat onto the dirt floor. Abe removed his armor, placed it neatly in the corner and sat on the mat.

Bayo sat beside him, on an even more worn mat, as Toki brought out a bowl of dried fish.

"Here is some eja gbigbe for you to snack on while I prepare the ground-nut stew," Toki said.

"Mo dupe!" Abe said, thanking her.

Abe looked into the bowl. There were several small, dry, catfish in the large, wooden bowl. A slender stick skewered each fish, forming them into circles. Abe removed a stick from one of the fish and then cracked the dry, brown flesh open with his hands. The Herald removed the fish's tiny spine and then began to carefully pull the meat from around the small, brittle bones. Bayo did the same with his fish, devouring the salty meat in large bites.

"Will you be competing in that tournament everyone is talking about?" Bayo asked.

"Actually, I have come to postpone it," Abe replied.

"Postpone it?" Bayo said, his eyes widening in shock. "Please forgive me if I speak out of turn, my Lord, but the tournament will bring much money and glory to Oyo. Why postpone it?"

"This is your home, citizen and I am your guest. You do not speak out of turn," Abe replied. "The Aare Ona Kakanfo is fighting to protect our lands from the savage Urabi. Of course, he is sure to win, just as he is sure to attain victory in the tournament, which is why we must postpone it until he returns from battle."

"A win by the Aare Ona Kakanfo in the Grand Tournament will bring even more of the glory of which you spoke and will solidify—in the minds of our enemies and allies—the supreme power of the warriors of Oyo!"

"I understand, my Lord," Bayo said. "I wish I could attend the Grand Tournament. I love to watch fights! I am from a long lineage of wrestlers. In fact, I was once champion wrestler of all Ajaland."

"Oh, really?" Abe said, raising an eyebrow.

"Of course, I would be no match for the Aare Ona Kakanfo," Bayo said. "But, I was quite the fighter in my day!"

Toki brought out a steaming bowl of stew and sat it before Abe. "Bayo, let our esteemed guest enjoy his meal in peace! Your food awaits you in the bedroom. Come eat!"

"Dear, Abe and I are talking," Bayo said. "Bring my food out here, please."

"Oh, no, it is fine," Abe said. "We cannot disappoint a woman who is with child, citizen. She must always be found with a smile upon her face!"

Bayo rose from his mat, rolled it up and tossed the frayed mat over his shoulder. "Then, I guess I will bid you good night, my Lord."

"We will see you in the morning, my Lord," Toki said.

"Sleep well, citizens," Abe replied.

The couple walked toward the kitchen, disappearing into shadow and the Herald returned to his delicious meal of dried fish and ground-nut stew.

*   *   *

"Do you really think we should risk it?" Bayo whispered.

"Of course we should!" Toki whispered in reply. "Our ancestors have blessed us with a grand opportunity!"

"You're right," Bayo said, nodding his head. "With the Aare Ona Kakanfo out of the picture, I can *win* the Grand Tournament!"

"Yes...*and* marry the princess!" Toki said. "I will be her elder co-wife!"

"And we will live in luxury for the rest of our lives!" Bayo replied.

Toki clapped her hands gleefully. A sardonic smile spread across her face. "Get the black root, Bayo. We have work to do!"

*   *   *

"How could this happen?" Abe cried. "I must have pushed him too hard!"

Abe, Bayo and Toki stood over the corpse of Abe's horse. The steed lay on its side. Its tongue—distended from its gaping mouth—had turned a pale, pinkish-grey.

"A horse! I need a horse!" Abe shouted, his voice trembling in panic. "It is a two days' ride from here to Metropolitan Oyo and the tournament starts in less than a fortnight!"

"You have plenty time, then," Bayo said.

"No, citizen, I do *not!*" Abe replied. "It takes time to rearrange things of this magnitude…to house and feed our guests from other lands as compensation for their time…to appease the fighters…to keep the princess, Eṣuṣeeke, in check…I need a horse! Now!"

Abe paced back and forth, rubbing his chin as if in deep thought. He suddenly stopped pacing and whirled around to face Abe. "You can have *our* horse, my Lord!"

"Bayo, we need Kini to plow the field," Toki said. "It is nearly time to plant seed."

"Dear, a warrior of the Oyo Empire—and an Eṣo, no less—needs our help!" Bayo said. "Please, let's give Kini to him. The ancestors will bless us."

"Fine," Toki sighed. "Please, take *our* horse, my Lord."

"Can it make the journey?" Abe asked.

"Kini is just a plow mare, but she's strong and healthy," Bayo replied.

"Well, she'll have to do," Abe said. "Mo dupe, family! Please, bring her to me."

Bayo ran to the rear of the house. A few moments later, he returned with a muscular, young mare. "Here you go, my Lord. This is Kini."

Abe lifted his saddle from the back of his dead steed and tossed it onto Kini's back. The horse bucked in protest.

Bayo stroked Kini's thick neck, calming her. "Good girl," he crooned. "Abe is our friend, Kini. He is going to take good care of you."

The horse bowed her head, signaling that it was okay for Abe to mount her. The Eṣo strapped the saddle onto Kini's chest and back and then climbed on.

"Mo dupe again, citizens!" Abe said. "I will assure that you are rewarded abundantly for your kindness."

"It is an honor, my Lord," Toki said, bowing her head.

"Good day and God-speed," Abe said as he rode off.

When the Herald had ridden from view, Toki turned to her husband. "How much powder did you give Kini?"

"Half a root," Bayo replied.

"Good. Kini should drop dead in about twelve hours," Toki said. "The Eşo will be stranded somewhere within Igbo Bamişo."

"Poor fellow," Bayo chuckled. "There is no telling what the Bamişo are going to do to Abe."

"All that matters," Toki began. "Is that those mischievous little Iwin are going to stop him from postponing the Grand Tournament!"

"Agreed," Bayo said. "Well, I'm off. Kayode has his racehorse ready to go."

Toki kissed her husband's full lips. "Give my big brother a hug for me and thank him for the use of his horse."

"I will," Bayo said as he sprinted down the road.

"Ride safely, my love," Toki called. "And fight well!"

CHAPTER 24

Sighashri.

Translated as "Molten Earth" in Urabic, the continent lived up to its name, as the ground remained scorching hot— day in and day out—through every season.

The only cool region of Sighashri was the mountainous East Lands, comprised of the nations of Huan Chuan, Yojinaga and Padampong.

The Southlands—comprised of the nations of Urabin, Vashti-Shah, Ma-Iti, and Qanas—was the hottest region on the vast continent. Dominated culturally and religiously by the desert-dwelling Urabi, the people of the Southlands thrived in the harsh environment.

Jabbar, the Demon, and Jalili, the eunuch, stepped through the gate of Al-Nur: the village of the Hashashin—the shadowy guild of spies and assassins in service to the Emir of Urabin—which was located at the southern border, between Urabin and Vashti-Shah.

The gate of Al-Nur remained unlocked, unmanned and unsecured at all times, for only a fool or a madman would venture into Al-Nur with anything but the best of intentions. Any fool or madman would die a horrible death and would incur the same fate upon his entire bloodline.

Al-Nur was as quiet as the grave. A lone, massive, domed building of limestone loomed in the distance. A twisted, bronze spire rose out of the dome and climbed high into the sky. There was no other sign of architecture and no sign of life, but the Demon knew better.

After a brisk walk to the village square, Jabbar raised his right hand, signaling Jalili to stop.

"Slowly bend a knee and lower your gaze," Jabbar whispered as he dropped his right knee into the sandy ground. "No sudden movements and only *I* speak!"

Jalili nodded, as he knelt beside Jabbar.

The two men placed their palms to the earth and locked their gazes on the sand between their fingertips.

After a few moments of silence, the earth exploded all around them.

Hashashin leapt from their hiding places under the surface of the sand, landing in a circle around Jabbar and Jalili.

With his gaze glued to the ground before him, Jabbar could only make out the tan, leather, curly-toe boots worn by every member of the shadowy Al-Nur guild of assassins.

"Why have you come?" a raspy voice asked.

"We are in need of the services of Suffering's Bride," Jabbar replied.

"Suffering's Bride is our very best," the raspy voice hissed. "She will cost you much."

"I offer much," Jabbar said. "I offer you land, wealth and—most of all—a position of honor amongst the Urabi, not one of loathing and fear.

"Fear is an effective tool, general," the voice said. "You—of all people—should know this.

"I agree," Jabbar said. "However, I am sure you know that admiration and love are stronger, more powerful tools!"

The voice did not respond for a long while and then said: "Agreed. Now, tell us, how will you deliver on your offer?"

"The Urabi fall beneath Oya blades, spears and arrows," Jabbar replied. "With Suffering's Bride at my side, we will turn the tides of war and give the Emir the victory he so desires. In exchange, he will grant me control over a portion of the land that is now Oyo…land that I will turn over to you to rule."

After a brief pause, the voice responded: "Suffering's Bride is yours to command for now. Utilize her well!"

Another explosion rocked the village square and all of the curly-toe boots vanished. All, except one pair.

CHAPTER 25

Igbo Bamiṣo, The Forest of the Bamiṣo Clan, was quiet; serene.

Just as the Bamiṣo—a malevolent family of Iwin— liked it and worked hard to maintain.

The Iwin were among the forces of the seen and unseen that overwhelmed human beings since time immemorial. They were not, however, beings and spirits to be worshiped; nor were they ghosts or Egungun, who appeared once a year as masquerades.

Iwin were not part of the invisible essence of self, like the abiku spirits that often replaced babies in the womb and tormented parents with stillbirth or premature death after birth. The Iwin were none of those things. But they were, however, just as dreaded.

An Iwin could be so evil that to see it could mean the end of one's life. The Bamiṣo were exceptionally evil and feared even by other Iwin.

Abe marched through the forest.

As peaceful as the forest was, peace eluded him. The Herald had left Kini's corpse behind half a day ago, and he had begun walking in an easterly course toward Oyo. But two hours later, he arrived at the same spot where the horse had suddenly fallen dead. Again he followed the easterly course and, again, he found himself back where he started. Again he tried and received the same outcome…and again… and again!

Abe plopped down onto a fallen tree trunk and hung his head. Fighting back tears of frustration, Abe removed his armor and then took a drink from the water-skin Toki had given him for his journey.

He nearly spat the water out when he suddenly felt something soft and furry brush against his ankle..

Abe looked down at his feet. Sitting between them, staring up into Abe's face was a small creature that reminded Abe of a tailless colobus monkey. The creature had large, brown eyes set in its ebony, almost human face. It stood about two feet high and was covered, from crest to ankle, in white fur.

The little creature seemed to smile innocently as it brushed against Abe's leg again.

"I hope your day has fared better than mine, my little friend," Abe sighed.

Another brush of softness on his right ear caused Abe to snap his head in the direction of the sensation.

Sitting on the stump next to Abe was another monkey-creature.

"Oh, greetings, little fellow," Abe chuckled. "You startled me."

Another brush on his left ear…and yet, another monkey creature.

"Oh…umm…another one, eh?" Abe said, a bit nervously. "You must be a little family."

Another brush on his right arm. And another on his left.

Abe began to feel uneasy. He stood up and began to gather his armor and weapons. "I'll just be leaving you to your business now, my little friends."

A rustling sound came from behind Abe. He turned to see what the little monkey-creatures were up to and came face to face with what looked to Abe to be well over two hundred of the creatures, standing in ranks and smiling.

Abe put down his armor, but held his sword out in front of him, and began to back away. "I'll come back for my things later, my friends. Enjoy yourselves and, please, forgive my intrusion."

Suddenly, the creatures' smiles twisted into scowls and a great roar rose up in unison from their throats.

Abe turned on his heels and darted off into the forest. The creatures—all Iwin of the Bamiṣo clan—took off after him, half sprinting on all fours on the ground and the other half leaping and swinging through the trees.

CHAPTER 26

Ile Ogun was abuzz with excitement. The stone bleachers were filled to capacity with spectators of every hue and culture.

Women from far-away lands winked and batted their gray, blue, hazel and dark brown eyes at the warriors as they stretched and warmed up in the Warriors' Pen.

Akin sat among his fellow competitors, dressed in the Aare Ona Kakanfo's leopard skin apron and the Kakanfo's greaves and armbands, which were carved from ironwood and decorated with white and indigo beads. The beaded veil of the Kakanfo's crown concealed Akin's face.

In the Royal Terrace, the Alaafin sat in the front row, flanked on his left by his third and fourth wives, Temilola and Ajoke, respectively. On his right sat his Great Wife, Usiade, and his second wife, Winlawe. They were all matching in richly embroidered orange and brown garments of the finest lace.

Seated behind the Alaafin and his wives, were the Alaafin's eldest children: Ṣeeke, Tayewo and Kehinde. Baṣorun Temileke sat behind the children, with the ruler of Kas— Kentake Amanikhete— seated beside him.

The remaining seats in the Royal Terrace were filled with the seven Oyo Mesi: the rulers of the seven regions of the Oyo Empire, and their spouses. All were dressed exquisitely in garments befitting their lofty stations and rich, expertly crafted jewelry.

On the main floor, an orchestra of drummers, agogo players and ṣekere players delivered a pulse-pounding tune that had the crowd dancing in their seats.

At the center of the main floor was the Circle of Sand—the ring in which the warriors would soon meet. The Circle was constructed of smooth, interlocking thunderstones, which were hurled to earth from heaven by none other than the Orişa Şango.

A six-inch thick bed of white sand was packed into the twenty-foot diameter circle.

The Alaafin stood and walked to the edge of the Royal Terrace. "Oh, what a beautiful day to do battle!"

The spectators replied with deafening applause.

The Alaafin raised his hands high above his head and the crowd fell silent. "I, Alaafin Rogba Adewale, welcome you all! I would like to extend a special welcome to you powerful, strong and courageous warriors who sit before me! Welcome to Ile Ogun, this magnificent arena! Welcome to my beautiful kingdom!"

The Alaafin pointed his right hand at the Warriors' Pen. "Today, you fight for the hand of my daughter, Eşuşeeke ... Şeeke, please stand."

Eşuşeeke rose out of her chair. The princess' beauty and grace left the male spectators and warriors enamored and the women in admiration or envy.

"Not only is she a joy to look upon," the Alaafin began. "She is also intelligent...talented..."

"And rich!" Bayo whispered.

"So, do your best, warriors," the Alaafin said. "Fight your hardest. The prize is well worth it!"

Şeeke and the Alaafin took their seats as the crowd erupted in applause, whistles and joyous stomping.

Temileke rose and walked to the railing at the edge of the Royal Terrace, just as the Alaafin had done.

"Warriors...the rules!" Temileke shouted. "You will fight until one of you is rendered unconscious, is too injured to continue, or submits by yelling 'Oto, oto, oto,' or by slapping the ground three times if you are unable to speak. Is that understood?"

"Be'ni, Oluwo!" The warriors shouted. "Yes, my Lord!"

"Although the use of weapons *is* allowed in this tournament," Temileke began, "only non-lethal force is permitted."

Temileke pointed toward the fearsome Mino, who surrounded the Circle of Sand. "If *any* warrior employs lethal force, he will be beheaded by the Mino at dawn!"

Oṣogbesan closed his eyes and bit his bottom lip to conceal his contempt.

"Now, without further delay…" Temileke shouted. "Let the Grand Tournament begin!"

CHAPTER 27

"The first fight is between two warriors who promise to rouse the Egungun from their eternal places of rest, and incite them to storm the arena!" Temileke shouted.

Our first fighter hails from the grasslands of the beautiful country of Butulozabwei," Temileke said. "Standing as tall as two men and as broad as three…let us welcome to the Circle of Sand the Chitauri Slayer…the Grasslands Gargantuan…the Butulozabwei Bull…Nkohbo Busisiwe!"

Nkohbo sauntered to the north end of the Circle of Sand, to shouts of admiration, awe and disbelief that a man of such mountainous proportion even existed—let alone was fighting in the Grand Tournament.

"Fighting Nkohbo is the Baale of the village of Ijeti," Temileke said. "A man with mysterious power, he is the elder among the warriors and has come to bring some wisdom to the youth by way of his fists!"

The crowd laughed and applauded in response to Temileke's witty discourse.

"Stepping into the Circle of Sand…" Temileke continued. "Is the powerful…the enigmatic…Oṣogbesan!"

The spectators applauded as Oṣogbesan entered the Circle of Sand at the south end.

Temileke slowly and dramatically raised his right hand in the air, his fingertips pointing skyward. "Warriors…"

Temileke snapped his right arm downward, until his fingertips were pointing at the arena floor. "Fight!"

Nkohbo rushed forward...

Oṣogbesan reached into the pocket of his robe and withdrew a fistful of dark brown palm seeds.

Nkohbo threw a powerful combination of punches, aimed at

Oṣogbesan's chest and face.

Oṣogbesan parried and dodged the strikes, allowing them to slip by harmlessly. He then tossed the seeds into the air. Nkohbo's huge fist hammered into Oṣogbesan's chest, sending the old man rolling backward across the ring.

Oṣogbesan slipped a small, wooden flute from the folds of his robe as he rolled into a kneeling position.

The marble-sized seeds rained down, pounding tiny craters into the sand. A single seed struck Nkohbo on the crest of his bald head. The seed bounced off of the giant's head and then landed in the sand.

Nkohbo studied the seeds, which lay on the ground around him. He then threw his head back and began to laugh. The spectators joined in, laughing at Oṣogbesan's feeble attack.

Oṣogbesan began to play a slow, soothing tune on his flute. The seeds burst open. Green smoke billowed from them.

The laughter abruptly ceased.

The smoke cleared.

Surrounding Nkohbo stood a score of warriors with flesh of hard bark. Their sinewy frames were spider-webbed by veins that were formed by a network of roots. Each Seed-Warrior was armed with a wooden spear. The creatures stood nearly as tall as Nkohbo, but were lean and wiry.

Nkohbo's eyes grew as wide as young calabashes at the sight of the Seed-Warriors, who stood, with an upright military posture, in ranks. The giant threw up his hands and screamed: "Oto! Oto! *Oto!*"

Oṣogbesan stopped playing his flute and slipped it back into his robe.

The Seed-Warriors disintegrated into dust.

The arena was silent for a few heartbeats and then it erupted into applause. Oṣogbesan stepped to the center of the Circle of Sand.

Nkohbo lumbered to the center of the Circle with his eyes fixed on the ground. The giant's heart pumped wildly and his hands trembled.

In the Royal Terrace, the Alaafin was on his feet, applauding. "Magnificent!"

"A *wizard* is in the Grand Tournament," Usiade

gasped. "This competition is going to be *very* interesting, indeed!"

Temileke raised his hands above his head and the crowd fell silent. "The winner—and moving on to the semi finals—is the wizard… Oşogbesan!"

Oşogbesan raised his right fist in victory. Nkohbo shuffled back to the Warriors' Pen.

Şeeke looked down at Akin, trying to conceal her worry with a smile. "A *wizard?!*" She said, under her breath. "Stay strong, my love!"

CHAPTER 28

Temileke gently squeezed Kentake Amanikhete's hand. "Kondo's time has come. Are you nervous?"

"Not at all," the Kentake replied. "Kundo—and Kas—shall be victorious!"

Temileke kissed the Kentake's hand and rose from his seat. "We shall see."

Temileke stepped up to the edge of the Royal Terrace. "Citizens, visitors, friends and friendly rivals…our second fight promises to be as exciting as the first!"

The Başorun pointed to the north end of the Circle of Sand. "Entering the Circle is a man that stands out among a people, that are known throughout Onile for their incredible prowess in wrestling: the Nuba of Kas. This wrestler is so skilled…so powerful…that the Kentake of Kas, Her Majesty, Amanikhete, has come to cheer him on to victory! Welcome…to the Circle of Sand…Kondo, of Kas!"

The crowd cheered as Kondo, covered from head-to-toe in a paste made of white clay, stepped into the Circle.

"And now…his opponent," Temileke continued. "Hailing from…parts unknown, was discovered by our magnanimous host, Alaafin Rogba Adewale!"

Temileke pointed toward the Circle's south end. A hunched figure—dressed in tattered, mud-stained clothing and worn sandals—limped into the Circle. The pathetic creature's face and hands were covered in layers of soiled strips of cloth, once white, now gray with filth.

A murmuring spread across the crowded arena. Gasps and cries of shock, empathy and disgust echoed throughout Ile Ogun.

"Please, do not look upon our brutish friend with pity," Temileke said. "It is rumored that this poor creature has killed more men than a dog has teeth!"

The crowd fell silent at Temileke's words. "Fear him…be in awe of him…show your appreciation for Omobe…'the Wrestler with a Thousand Scars!'"

The crowd cheered. A few turned up their noses in repugnance.

Kondo bent his knees deeply and bent slightly forward at the waist. His open palms moved in a smooth, elliptical motion in front of his chest.

Omobe pressed his palms against the sides of his scrap-covered head and lifted his left knee to his chest, with his left foot extended out toward his left hip. The beastly, little man supported himself on his right leg, which was slightly bent at the knee.

"Fight!" Temileke commanded.

Kondo leapt forward, his hands reaching for Omobe's waist. Omobe spun to his right as he whipped his left leg toward Kondo's head.

Omobe's shin crashed into the side of Kondo's neck. The stunned Kondo dropped to his knees.

Omobe skipped toward Kondo and launched a flying knee strike at his face.

Kondo regained his composure and, with blinding speed, grabbed Omobe around the waist with both arms.

Kondo squeezed Omobe's pelvis toward him as he drove his head into Omobe's chest. The powerful pull-push action deeply arched the scarred wrestler's back, throwing him off balance.

Kondo exploded forward as he increased the pressure on Omobe's pelvis.

Omobe's back slammed onto the ground. A coarse cloud of sand billowed up from the ground.

Kondo knelt between Omobe's legs. He threw a flurry of punches, striking Omobe several times in the ribs and jaw.

The Wrestler with a Thousand Scars deflected a right hook punch past his face with his left hand, and then wrapped his right leg around the back of Kondo's neck.

Omobe threw his left leg over his right foot, trapping Kondo's neck and right arm in a tight 'figure-four' choke with his legs. Omobe forced Kondo's head toward his abdomen, utilizing a strong, downward push with his hands. The constriction around Kondo's neck tightened even more.

Kondo's eyes reddened and nearly bulged out of their sockets. A string of saliva trickled from the Nuba wrestler's distended tongue.

Kondo's body shook wildly for a few moments and then went limp.

Omobe pushed Kondo's unconscious body off of him.Kondo fell onto his face with a dull thud. Omobe rolled to his feet and then slowly shambled back toward the Warriors' Pen.

"An amazing match!" Temileke exclaimed. "The winner—and next semi-finalist—is Omobe, the Wrestler with a Thousand Scars!"

Temileke returned to his seat beside Kentake Amanikhete as a quartet of young men rolled the still unconscious Kondo onto a blanket and carried him out of the Circle of Sand.

"What now?" Temileke whispered to the Kentake.

"Now, *you* had better be as good a man as I think you are, or this trip will have been a total waste of time," Kentake Amanikhete replied.

"I promise, Your Majesty," Temileke began. "You will return to Kas with barely an inkling of the loss your champion suffered here today."

The Kentake laid a hand upon Temileke's knee. Her touch was soft, warm...yet a delicious chill ran up the Başorun's spine.

"The memory is fading already," Kentake Amanikhete whispered.

* * *

In the bleachers, on the main floor, Master Gboyega raised an eyebrow. Although he had never seen—or heard of —the Wrestler with a Thousand Scars, Omobe seemed strangely...familiar.

The old warrior could not put his finger on it yet, but he was sure that clarity would come to him *very soon*.

CHAPTER 29

Akin sat alone, at the top row of the bleachers in the Warriors' Pen.

Bayo hopped onto the bench Akin occupied and then slid close to him. "So, how are you doing, Kakanfo?" Bayo asked. "Umm…you *are* the Aare Ona Kakanfo, aren't you?"

"Of course I am, citizen," Akin replied, keeping up the lie. "Why would you ask such a foolish question of your Aare Ona Kakanfo?"

"Well, sir, I am just curious how you are *here* when you sent your Herald, Abe, on a mission from the northern border to postpone the tournament until you arrive."

"I used magic, of course!" Akin said.

"No, you did not," Bayo snickered. "But, do not fret. Your secret is safe with me…as long as you do me a big favor."

"What is the favor?" Akin sighed, raising an eyebrow.

"If we meet in the Circle of Sand, you lose!"

"Are you out of your *mind*?" Akin spat. "I *do not* lose!"

"You will lose your *head* if they find out you're an imposter *and* wearing the regalia of someone who is above your station," Bayo said.

"And what if we don't meet in the Circle?" Akin asked.

"Then, that crown is mine," Bayo replied. "There are collectors here from other lands that would pay an obscenely large sum in cowries for it."

Temileke stepped to the edge of the Royal Terrace.

"Do we have a deal?" Bayo asked. Akin nodded in reply.

"And now…our third fight!" Temileke exclaimed. "This fighter is a citizen of the Oyo Empire—from the layer of Ajaland—and a former wrestling champion…"

Bayo stared at Akin as he drew a gauntlet from his buba. The gauntlet was constructed of a material Akin had never before seen. It was metallic, yet slipped onto Bayo's arm like silk.

The jet-black glove seemed to pulse as Bayo curled his fingers into a fist. The gauntlet tightened around Bayo's forearm and hand, molding to the limb like a metallic, second skin.

"Give a rousing round of applause for...*Bayo!*" Temileke shouted.

Bayo leapt from the bleachers and danced his way into the Circle of Sand, shaking his armored fist above his head and grinding his hips lewdly in a circular motion.

The crowd cheered. Many women whistled and several tossed cowry shells or pieces of gold at Bayo's feet.

"O...kay," Temileke snickered. "Ladies and gentlemen, let's welcome to the ring the Destroyer of Armies...the Slayer of Gods... the Terror of the Kongo...Runihara!"

Runihara stood on the bench upon which he sat, bent his stubby legs and then exploded upward.

The stout, little man sailed through the air and then landed in the center of the Circle of Sand, mere inches from Bayo.

"Fight!" Temileke ordered.

Bayo struck first, driving a devastating uppercut into Runihara's solar plexus.

The power of Bayo's gauntlet became painfully apparent as Runihara flew back into the Warriors' Pen, landing with a crunching thud as his back slammed into one of the stone benches at the apex of the bleachers.

Bayo raised his hands in victory. A toothy grin spread from cheek-to-cheek. His eyes filled with tears of joy.

This quickly turned into tears of anguish as an incisive pain coursed through his head and a tearing at the flesh and bone threatened to bifurcate his skull at mid-brow. Bayo looked up toward the source of his pain.

Runihara's maw was stretched open to monstrous proportions, like a python swallowing the hindquarters of a yearling calf.

Runihara's bottom row of steel, shark-like teeth bit into Bayo's forehead. The little man's top row of teeth dug into Bayo's occiput. Blood trickled down the front and back of Bayo's skull, spotting his neck, shoulders and face crimson.

Runihara's legs were extended outward horizontally, his body suspended in mid-air and straight as a board. Runihara threw a storm of hook punches into Bayo's temple and jaw.

Darkness crept up Bayo's spine and slithered around his consciousness.

The former wrestling champion reached up with his gloved hand and grabbed Runihara's neck. He then squeezed, putting tremendous pressure on the sides of Runihara's neck with his fingers and thumb and on the little man's throat with the web between his thumb and index finger.

The tiny terror coughed up a misty cloud of blood.

Bayo squeezed harder as unconsciousness overcame him. He toppled backward, his hand still locked around Runihara's thick neck.

Bayo's back—and the top of Runihara's head— slammed onto the sand covered ground.

Both men lay still.

The crowd was silent.

The Alaafin looked over his shoulder at Temileke, whose eyes were wide with surprise.

A brief examination by Baba Fafore determined the two fighters were unconscious, not dead. Baba Fafore gave thrust both thumbs upward in confirmation of life.

The Alaafin waved his hand, signaling Temileke to come to him.

Temileke rose from his seat and briskly approached the Alaafin. The Başorun bent at the waist, bringing his ear close to the Alaafin's lips.

The Alaafin whispered into Temileke's ear.

Temileke smiled and nodded in approval. He stepped to the edge of the Royal Terrace and raised his hands. "Since both fighters have rendered each other unconscious, His Imperial Highness has declared this match a *draw*!"

The crowd cheered, as both fighters were carried off the mat and taken back to the Warriors' Pen to be attended to by Baba Fafore's team of Babalawo and Iyanifa.

"*Both* fighters will move on to the semi-finals," Temileke said.

Temileke pointed toward Oṣogbesan, who sat off to himself in the Warriors' Pen. "And since the wizard, Oṣogbesan, has certain…*advantages*…he will fight Bayo *and* Runihara!"

The crowd roared with excitement.

"Can you handle that, Oṣogbesan?" Temileke asked.

Chief Oṣogbesan nodded, and then interlaced his fingers behind his head as if he did not have a care in the world. "No problem, Baṣorun. No problem at all."

CHAPTER 30

"And now…the final match to determine our last semi-finalist!" Temileke said. "Coming to the Circle of Sand…this fighter hails from the plains of Kirinyaga. 'The Hunter, who hunts the Lion alone'…the Maasai Moran…Nangwaya!"

The spectators cheered.

Nangwaya strutted to the center of the ring, his red robe waving loosely against his wiry frame with each step.

The warrior began to leap high into the air—keeping his legs as straight as the wooden spear he carried—in the traditional dance of the Maasai Moran.

"Now, entering the Circle of Sand, is a man who really needs no introduction," Temileke shouted. "Hailing from the Warriors' Complex of Metropolitan Oyo…he is the War Chief of War Chiefs… the Commander of the mighty military machine of the Oyo Empire…a blood descendant of the Orişa Şango, himself! The Aare Ona Kakanfo… Ibikunle Şangodele!"

The lion's share of the crowd leapt to their feet, clapping, stomping and whistling fervently as Akin sauntered into the Circle of Sand.

Akin drew his ironwood swords from the sheaths that were strapped to his back.

The crowd roared even louder.

"Fight!" Temileke commanded.

Nangwaya lunged forward, thrusting his spear at Akin's right foot.

Akin slid his foot backward, avoiding the strike. He then swung the broad side of the sword he held in his right hand at Nangwaya's face.

The wooden weapon smacked Nangwaya in the jaw.

The Maasai stumbled backward.

Akin leapt forward, his swords raised high above his head.

Nangwaya leapt backward as he swung his spear in a wide arc. The shaft of the spear hammered into Akin's ribcage.

Akin fell to the ground. His side felt as if it had been struck by a mad bull. He struggled to his feet, fighting to block out the pain.

Nangwaya charged forward, thrusting the blunted point of his spear at Akin's chest.

Akin spun to his left, evading the spear and then— utilizing the momentum of his spin—whipped a powerful right round-kick, in a downward arc, toward Nangwaya's left thigh.

Nangwaya slammed the pommel of his spear into the sand in an attempt to form a barrier between his leg and Akin's kick.

Akin's shin struck the shaft of Nangwaya's spear with fearsome force. The spear shattered into tiny slivers and dust.

Akin's shin continued in its downward arc, pounding into Nangwaya's thigh. The Maasai Moran screamed as his left femur snapped.

Akin's kick continued its terrible course even further, driving Nangwaya's fractured left thigh into his right leg.

The Maasai's right femur collapsed outward with a sickening crack. Nangwaya fell to the ground, rolling from side-to-side in agony.

Akin saluted his downed opponent and then sheathed his swords.

"The winner…and last semi-finalist is…Ibikunle Ṣangodele… the Aare Ona Kakanfo!" Temileke shouted.

Ṣeeke leapt from her chair, clapping her hands gleefully. "Incredible match, Kakanfo! *Incredible!*"

The Alaafin and Usiade exchanged glances. "When did Ṣeeke become such a fan of the Aare Ona Kakanfo?" Usiade asked.

"I have no clue," the Alaafin replied with a shrug. "Perhaps she finds a man who fractures the thigh bones of another man appealing."

"Perhaps," Usiade said, shaking her head.

"We now have all of our semi-finalists," Temileke said. "Two will go on to fight for the coveted championship and the hand of the lovely princess, Ṣeeke!"

The crowd cheered and whistled.

"We will now take a brief intermission," Temileke said. "So, talk among yourselves, get something to eat and shop in our beautiful marketplace…"

"What about the wenches?" Someone shouted from among the spectators.

"Wenches?" Temileke said, turning up his nose in disdain. "This isn't Celtshire, friend. Touch our women, or proposition them inappropriately and the only hole you will enjoy is the one we bury you in!"

Many among the spectators—especially the women—leapt to their feet, cheering wildly.

"Be back in your seats by mid-day," Temileke continued. "You do *not* want to miss a *second* of the spectacular semi-finals!"

CHAPTER 31

The crowd had returned to Ile Ogun.

Their money was well-spent. Their bellies, well-fed, their fervor—as intense as the noon-day heat.

The children, and some adults, in the arena held up hand-carved, wooden effigies of their favorite fighters—with the Oşogbesan and 'Kakanfo' figurines being the most popular.

Temileke stepped to the edge of the Royal Terrace. "Citizens… guests…warriors and royalty…welcome to the semi-finals of the greatest tournament in the history of man!"

Ile Ogun erupted in applause and cheers.

"Our first semi-final fight will be retold in song, and in fireside chats, throughout eternity and around the world," Temileke said, drawing a huge circle in the air with his outstretched hands. "Let us welcome to the ring Runihara, Bayo and the wizard, Baale Oşogbesan!"

Runihara and Bayo sprinted into the north end of the Circle of Sand. Oşogbesan strolled calmly into the Circle of Sand at the south end.

"Fight!" Temileke shouted.

Bayo and Runihara—running side-by-side—charged the wizard.

Oşogbesan snatched a fistful of seeds from a pocket in his robes and flung them into the sand. He withdrew his flute from a pocket hidden within the folds of his robe and brought the instrument to his lips.

A seering pain, however, radiating from Oşogbesan's neck to his right wrist, stopped the wizard from playing a note.

Runihara's steel shark teeth were buried in Oşogbesan's shoulder.

Runihara sank his teeth deeper. The wizard screamed as sinew and bone were torn and pulverized.

The flute fell from Oṣogbesan's fingers and landed at his feet.

As Oṣogbesan struggled to push Runihara's mouth from his severely wounded shoulder, Bayo punched the wizard in the sternum.

The powerful strike, amplified five-fold by Bayo's gauntlet, sent Oṣogbesan flying backward. The wizard landed on his side and skittered across the sand and out of the Circle, coming to rest at the feet of the drummers.

Oṣogbesan coughed up blood as he struggled to his knees. His right arm hung lifelessly at his side.

"Stay down, old man," Bayo shouted. "You cannot beat us *both!*"

Runihara licked a drop of Oṣogbesan's blood from his lips. Mmm…you taste *good*, wizard! Fight more, so I can *taste* more!"

Oṣogbesan extended his palm toward his flute, which lay at the center of the Circle of Sand.

"Dide! Dide! Dide!" the wizard shouted in rapid succession, commanding his instrument to rise.

The flute sped along the surface of the sand and then launched into the air. The magic instrument flew into Oṣogbesan's waiting palm.

The wizard played a quick, staccato tune.

The palm seeds erupted into smoke. Out of the smoke, a wooden spear struck Bayo in the head. Another hit Runihara on his back.

The smoke cleared and Oṣogbesan's opponents found themselves surrounded by a score of Seed-Warriors.

The Seed-Warriors brutally pounded Runihara and Bayo about the head, legs, back and arms with rapid, stinging strikes.

Runihara and Bayo screamed, almost in unison: "Oto! Oto! *Oto!*" The crowd laughed as Bayo and Runihara dashed from the Circle of Sand and back to the Warriors' Pen.

Oṣogbesan—still on his knees—held up his flute in triumph.

"The winner…" Temileke began, "and first finalist is … Oṣogbesan!"

Oṣogbesan struggled to his feet and then walked back to the Warriors' Pen to the roaring adulation of the spectators.

"Great fight!" Akin said, smiling and extending his left hand toward Oṣogbesan.

Oṣogbesan stared at Akin's hand as if it was covered in feces. He then pushed Akin's hand to the side. The wizard sat down in the Warriors' Pen, never speaking a word.

"Be sure to see a healer about that arm and rest well, wizard!" Akin spat. "I want you at your *best* when you face me in the finals!"

Omobe leapt into a handstand, balancing himself on the back of a stone bench. "It is *I* the wizard shall face, Kakanfo! Omobe shall be victorious!"

"I am about to beat you like you stole my goat, Omobe," Akin sneered.

Omobe—still balanced on his hands—pounced onto the seat next to Akin. "Omobe shall take no beatings!"

"Oh, you won't have to *take* it," Akin replied. "I'm going to *give* it to you!"

Omobe executed an aerial cartwheel to the floor of the Warriors' Pen. "We shall see soon."

"One more 'shall' from that little monster and I will scream!" Oṣogbesan said, rolling his eyes.

"No, no..." Akin replied. "You *shall* scream."

The competitors laughed. Oṣogbesan crossed his arms on his chest and turned sideways on his bench, offering his back to Akin. "Humph!" he snorted.

CHAPTER 32

"And now…the final match to decide which warrior will fight Oşogbesan in the finals!" Temileke shouted. "Will it be…Omobe, the 'Wrestler with a Thousand Scars'?"

Omobe entered the ring executing a series of somersaults and aerial twists. The hunched, little man landed in a one-handed handstand.

The crowd roared.

"Or will it be the Aare Ona Kakanfo?"

Akin swaggered into the Circle of Sand to thunderous applause. Even behind the veil of the Aare Ona Kakanfo's crown, it was clear that Akin grinned with confidence.

Omobe looked up at the Royal Terrace. The Alaafin sat back in his seat, relaxed— sure that his favored fighter, the Aare Ona Kakanfo, would win. Şeeke seemed strangely happy with the Kakanfo's performance, almost as if she was enamored with him.

But, Şeeke had no clue what kind of man the Kakanfo really was. The Aare Ona Kakanfo could be a cruel bastard and did not deserve a genuinely good woman like Şeeke.

To hell with the Alaafin, Omobe thought. *The Aare Ona Kakanfo will* lose *this day!*

Akin assumed a low, crouched fighting stance.

Omobe remained balanced on his right arm.

"Fight!" Temileke ordered.

Akin spun backward, to his left, as he extended his right leg. His muscular leg whipped around toward Omobe's right elbow.

Omobe pushed off his arm, launching himself backward, away from Akin's spinning reap-kick.

Akin sprang from the ground and leapt toward Omobe, who was still sailing backward in the air.

Omobe landed on his feet and then immediately rebounded—

like a rubber ball—toward Akin.

The Wrestler with a Thousand Scars slammed the top of his head into Akin's solar plexus. The air exploded from Akin's lungs.

Akin drove the tip of his left elbow between Omobe's shoulder-blades.

Akin collapsed onto his knees, gasping for air.

Omobe fell onto all fours, fighting back the encroaching darkness of unconsciousness.

Akin recovered first. He burst forward, wrapping his left arm around the back of Omobe's neck and then pulling his left wrist-bone into Omobe's throat with his right hand.

Omobe pulled down on Akin's left arm, in order to gain enough room to turn his head toward Akin's left side, greatly diminishing the crushing pressure of the guillotine choke.

The Wrestler with a Thousand Scars shuffled around to Akin's left side, reached between Akin's legs with both hands and then drove his forearms up into 'the Kakanfo's' groin.

Akin's knees wobbled and his legs became as flimsy as rice noodles.

Omobe lifted Akin high into the air by his crotch and then slammed the back of Akin's head into the ground.

Akin's world faded to gray and then into total blackness. Omobe released Akin's unconscious body, letting it fall to the ground with a loud *flump*.

In the Royal Terrace, a tear fell from Şeeke's right eye and raced down her cheek.

The Alaafin held his head in shock.

Let's see if you look so pompous now, Omobe thought, peeking under the Aare Ona Kakanfo's veil.

"A-Akin?" Omobe whispered upon seeing Akin's face under the veil. "What have I done?"

"The Wrestler with a Thousand Scars" nearly cried out in her real voice. The voice of Mistress Oyabakin.

Mistress Oyabakin drove her thumbs into pressure points on the insides of Akin's thighs. Akin began to stir back to consciousness.

Oyabakin pressed another point on Akin's left shoulder. Akin's left arm flew out in a weak straight punch, which glanced Mistress Oyabakin's jaw.

The War-Mistress threw herself backward and landed on her side. She grabbed her face, screaming in affected agony. Akin rose to his feet, confused and a bit dazed.

Mistress Oyabakin shook wildly and then lay still.

After a long silence, the arena filled with thundering applause. The Alaafin and Şeeke seemed to clap and cheer louder than everyone else in the arena.

Akin shrugged and then raised his hands in victory.

"What an incredible and somewhat...strange victory!" Temileke said. "Just when we thought it was over for the Aare Ona Kakanfo, he amazed us all and defeated Omobe! *That*, my friends, is why Ibikunle Şangodele is the Warlord of Warlords!"

Akin returned to the Warriors' Pen, still unsure just *how* he won the match.

Mistress Oyabakin "struggled" to her feet and then limped toward the ramp leading from the Warriors' Pen to the surface.

Suddenly, a strong hand grabbed Mistress Oyabakin's arm. She recognized the aşe in the grip. It belonged to her husband.

"You look *hurt*," Master Gboyega said. "Let me help you to your seat, *Omobe*!"

"Let me explain," Oyabakin whispered.

"No need," Master Gboyega replied. "I already know. The Alaafin wanted you to ensure the Aare Ona Kakanfo makes it to the finals, correct?"

"Yes."

"Problem is...that is *not* the Aare Ona Kakanfo!" Master Gboyega hissed. "*That* is our son!"

"Yes," Mistress Oyabakin sighed, lowering her gaze.

"What are you two up to?" Gboyega asked.

"I did not know Akin was posing as the Aare Ona Kakanfo,"

Mistress Oyabakin replied. "I discovered it after I knocked him unconscious."

"The Alaafin will have Akin executed once His Imperial Highness realizes what Akin has done," Master Gboyega said. "Win or lose, after the finals, our son must leave Oyo forever!"

CHAPTER 33

"Two great warriors are about to meet in this arena of earth and sand and stone," Temileke said, shaking his fists. "Two great warriors will—on this day— make history and will be praised, forevermore, by Jeli, Ijala, Sanusi and Sesh alike."

The drummers began to play a slow, stirring song that shook the arena.

Master Gboyega sauntered into the center of the Circle of Sand. "As is customary at gatherings of warriors in Oyo, we tell stories of our warrior-ancestors. This honor has been bestowed upon me at this most august meeting of hearts, minds and bodies. I would like to share a story of the blind princess, Efunlade, the mother of my wife, Mistress Oyabakin.

The spectators grew silent. They sat forward in their seats, giving Master Gboyega their undivided attention as he told them the story of "The Lesson on Itase Hill"…

* * *

"Damn, it is colder than an Urabi's heart up here!" Fakoya said as he briskly rubbed his muscular arms with his iron-rod fingers. "You really should have stayed home."

Fakoya peered over his shoulder at his wife, Efunlade. Her long, thick braids—excited by the icy wind—danced seductively on her sinewy shoulders.

The mahogany-hued beauty leaned into the whipping wind as she tapped on the loose, white rocks of Itase Hill with her walking stick. "*You* really should be *quiet* and reserve your energy. You are going to *need* it."

"Humph," Fakoya grunted. "I am going to pound the White Warrior into dust and still have enough energy to make incredible love to you come nightfall!"

Efunlade laughed. Her honey-sweet laughter was like music and sweetened the bitter cackle of the hill winds.

"Come here, Fakoya," Efunlade said. "I want to feel that haughty expression on your face."

Fakoya sauntered over to his wife. His broad shoulders swayed and dipped with each slow, measured step. The giant's crimson vest clung to his steely upper back and the thick leather swelled against the pressure of his massive chest.

Efunlade gently caressed Fakoya's thick jaw and high cheekbones with her long, smooth fingers. Fakoya's face spoke volumes to Efunlade's hands.

"Mm-hmm...*haughty*!" Efunlade giggled. "You are so adorable when you are convinced that you cannot lose."

Efunlade stood on the tips of her toes, craned her neck as far as she could and then planted a soft kiss on Fakoya's thick neck.

The giant smiled and then drew his Oṣe Ṣango—his double-bladed axe—from its red and white leather sheath. The handle was as thick as the trunk of a palm sapling and each blade was as broad as a man's torso.

The man-monolith slammed the pommel of the axe-handle into the alabaster earth. The dry, white soil cracked and crumbled under the tremendous weight of the axe. The hillside shook and the air rumbled like the sound of distant, rolling thunder.

"White Warrior!" Fakoya shouted. "Fakoya is coming for you!"

Fakoya's voice echoed across the hills and valleys that comprised the city of Ife. Oke Itase, the tallest hill in Onile, loomed high above the other hills; and was rumored to be the home of the famed White Warrior—a powerful fighter who had remained undefeated for three generations.

"Subtlety is definitely not your strong suit," Efunlade said, shaking her head.

Fakoya's powerful shoulders shook as he threw back his head and chortled with abandon. "Come on, laughing man," Efunlade said as she resumed the trek up the hill. "Let's get you to the top of this hill!"

Fakoya hoisted his axe onto his right shoulder and skipped briskly behind his wife. Efunlade shook her head and did her best to tune out the *"skff-skff-skff"* of Fakoya's skipping steps. She was quite sure her giant of a husband looked quite silly, skipping along like a happy village schoolboy.

* * *

The summit of Itase Hill was stark white.

The wild grass, the thick twisted iroko trees, which kissed the crisp afternoon sky—even the furry colobus monkeys, that leapt from treetop to treetop and the powerful rams that darted through the dense forest— were all pristine white.

"Efunlade," Fakoya gasped. "I-I have never seen *any*thing like *this*!"

"Is it beautiful?" Efunlade asked.

"It is…it…" Suddenly, Fakoya felt dizzy and the words choked in his throat.

Everything seemed to meld together in the all-encompassing whiteness of the forested hilltop. Fakoya could no longer discern tree from monkey, monkey from rock, rock from ram.

Waves of nausea bubbled up from Fakoya's somersaulting gut. He closed his eyes and sucked in large gulps of cold, mountain air.

"Fakoya?" Efunlade called as she reached out to her husband. "Are you okay?"

Fakoya clenched his fists, sucked in one last, deep breath and then slowly opened his eyes. The nausea and the dizziness were gone. "I am fine, love. I am going to find the White Warrior and bring him here for our match. Sit tight. You should be safe here."

Fakoya kissed Efunlade's outstretched palms and then sprinted into the dense, white forest.

Suddenly, the dizziness returned. The giant stumbled and fell to his knees. The bubbling waves of nausea rose again and erupted in a forceful spray of vomit, which splashed onto the white grass. The sputum slowly sank into the pigmentless soil until there was no trace of it and the grass was, once again, pure white.

Fakoya struggled to his feet, fighting off the whirling sickness in his belly. He turned on his heels and stumbled back toward where he had left Efunlade.

As he got closer to where his wife was waiting, he heard singing...

"Oro la yangba,
Oro la yangba,
A yo gege Balorun leyo
Oro la yangba o,
A yo gege Balorun leyo
Oro la yangba o
A yo gege Balorun leyo
Oro la yangba o.
Orişanla o
A la gogo de o
O dan o jelala ofilala ofilolo
Obatala o
A la gogo de o
O dan o jelala ofilala ofilolo
O dan o jelala
Ofilala
Ofilolo."

The giant picked up his pace. He had heard this song before. The song of the White Warrior.

As Fakoya neared the resting place of his wife, he realized the song was coming from her lips.

Fakoya paused as Efunlade came into view. She was standing

in the center of a circle of white stones. Her walking cane lay at her feet.

> *"Obatala o*
> *A la gogo de o*
> *O dan o jelala ofilala ofilolo."*

"What is this, Efunlade?" Fakoya gasped. "You sing praises to my rival?"

Efunlade knelt in the center of the white stone circle. "Fakoya, it is time."

Fakoya laughed. "Wait…you want me to believe that *you* are the legendary White Warrior of Itase Hill?"

Efunlade smiled warmly. "It is time, love. Shall we begin?"

Fakoya's laughter faded. His smile contorted into a scowl. "*Enough*, woman! Let's go home!"

Efunlade rested her hands on her lap.

> *"Obatala o*
> *A la gogo de o*
> *O dan o jelala ofilala ofilolo."*

Fakoya leapt into the circle of stones. He landed in front of his kneeling wife with a loud thud. The soft, white soil sank beneath his feet.

Fakoya knelt before his wife and swung his huge right palm toward Efunlade's cheek. The blind woman deflected the blow with her right hand, and then struck Fakoya in the cheek with a whipping backhand slap.

White-hot needles of pain radiated across Fakoya's reddening face.

The giant shook off the pain and threw a strong left, straight punch toward Efunlade's nose. Efunlade ensnared the strike with her left hand, which coiled around his arm like a python encircling its prey.

Efunlade forcefully jerked Fakoya forward and then slammed

her right wrist-bone into the side of her husband's neck. Fakoya's vision blurred and his arms fell limply at his sides.

Efunlade followed with a powerful right punch that slammed into Fakoya's solar plexus.

The giant slid backward on his knees, stopping a few yards outside the circle. Fakoya struggled to regain the breath that had abandoned him.

Efunlade rolled to her feet, pounced toward Fakoya and landed softly and silently in front of him. The White Warrior stroked her husband's massive shoulders and planted a soft kiss on his forehead.

Air rushed back into Fakoya's lungs as his shoulders shook while he cried. Tears rolled down Fakoya's cheeks, dripped onto his vest and ran—in rivulets—down to his lap.

The giant looked up at his wife, who smiled warmly down at him. "I have much to learn," he cried. "Please, teach me."

"Oh, my husband," Efunlade said, as she gently caressed Fakoya's face. "If you treat me with respect, I will teach you everything I know."

* * *

The crowded arena trembled from the applause and stomps that followed Master Gboyega's tale. Master Gboyega bowed slightly at the waist and then left the Circle of Sand.

Suddenly, an undulating cloak of thick darkness engulfed the Circle of Sand. "Citizens…guests…friends…" Temileke began. "We give you the mighty Aare Ona Kakanfo!"

A column of light descended from the sky and struck the Circle. Half of the darkness parted, revealing Akin, standing strong, with his ironwood swords at the ready.

Temileke pointed at the remaining darkness in the Circle of Sand. "And his opponent…the formidable Baale of Ijeti…Oṣogbesan!"

A second column of light descended and struck the remaining darkness. The darkness dissipated completely… revealing Oṣogbesan, standing with a fistful of palm seeds in his left hand and his flute in his right.

The wizard's right arm had fully recovered from Runihara's earlier assault, thanks to the expert healing work of Baba Fafore and his team.

"Fight!" Temileke shouted.

Oṣogbesan dropped the seeds in front of himself and began to play his flute. Akin exploded forward, launching himself in the air toward the wizard.

Suddenly, a wall of Seed-Warriors rose in front of Akin. The young warrior executed a quick backhanded slash with his left hand and a deep thrust with his right.

Akin's left sword decapitated a Seed-Warrior as his right sword pierced another's earthen heart. Both creatures disintegrated into a fine, red dust.

A Seed-Warrior thrust his spear at Akin's throat.

Akin leaned to his right to dodge the strike, but wasn't quite quick enough and the spear grazed his neck. A rivulet of blood ran down Akin's armored vest and fell, like crimson rain, in the sand.

Two Seed-Warriors thrust their spears at Akin's thighs in an attempt to sever his femoral arteries.

Akin jumped over the spears, bringing both of his knees to his chest. He then drove his heels downward, stepping on the spears and breaking them in half.

Akin lashed out with both swords, decapitating his attackers and again, red dust fell.

"Baba, you must stop this!" Ṣeeke cried. "Oṣogbesan is trying to *kill* the Kakanfo!"

"Yes, you are right," the Alaafin said. "Temileke, order Oṣogbesan to stand down at once and declare the Aare Ona Kakanfo the winner of this tournament!"

"Yes, Your Highness," Temileke replied with a bow.

Before Temileke could speak, however, a Seed-Warrior slashed at Akin's head.

Akin snapped his head backward, avoiding the deadly cut, but the Seed-Warrior's spearhead struck the veil of the Aare Ona Kakanfo's crown, rending it in two.

Beads rained onto the sand and that rain of beads washed away Akin's façade.

The Alaafin jumped out of his seat. "What in the *world?!* That is *not* the Aare Ona Kakanfo!"

"*What?*" Şeeke cried out in shock.

Temileke signaled the Mino.

The warrior-women surrounded Oşogbesan and Akin with their spears and swords prepared to attack at the slightest movement from either of them. No one dared defy the Mino— not even the most powerful wizards and the mightiest warriors. For they were women with fearsome aşe that enabled them to fight on both the physical and the spiritual planes simultaneously.

"Cease fighting, now!" Temileke commanded.

Oşogbesan stopped playing his flute. His Seed-Warriors disintegrated into dust and swirled away on gusts of wind.

Akin sheathed his swords.

The Alaafin walked to the edge of the Royal Terrace. Şeeke stood beside him. Their faces were twisted masks of anger, confusion and pain.

"That is *not* the Aare Ona Kakanfo!" The Alaafin shouted at the spectators. "That is Akinkugbe Ogunlade, son of Master Gboyega and Mistress Oyabakin! Arrest him *and* the wizard!"

Oyabakin—still in her guise of Omobe—yelled from the ramp leading from the Warriors' Pen to the surface. "You *need* to reconsider that decision, Your Highness. Let us all keep cool, for if it gets any hotter, I might have to remove my mask and reveal my...ugliness!"

"Umm...Omobe speaks wisely," the Alaafin said shakily. "However, *something* must be done. These men have committed..."

A sound, like rolling thunder resounded throughout Ile Ogun and the earthen walls trembled.

"What is happening *now*?" The Alaafin sighed.

"Horses, Your Highness," Master Gboyega replied. Approaching quickly!"

CHAPTER 34

Master Gboyega and the Emi Omo Eşo stood at the surface above Ile Ogun, weapons drawn and ready to meet the dark mass that thundered on the horizon.

The mass approached rapidly.

"Sheath your weapons and take a knee!" Master Gboyega ordered.

The Young Warriors did as instructed, kneeling in the traditional warriors' salute. The identity of the riders quickly became apparent: the Eşo, led by the Aare Ona Kakanfo.

The grandeur of the Eşo seemed diminished, however, as the elite warriors were battered, filthy and reeking of blood and death.

"Rise, warriors of Oyo!" The Kakanfo commanded. "Ready yourselves for battle *now!*"

Master Gboyega and the Emi Omo Eşo snapped to attention.

"I must address the Alaafin at once!" The Kakanfo said. "To the palace!"

"The Alaafin—and the Oyo Mesi—are below us, in Ile Ogun, My Lord," Master Gboyega said.

"The arena?" The Kakanfo asked, frowning in confusion. "Wasn't the tournament postponed?"

"No, my Lord," Gboyega replied.

"Where is Abe?" The Kakanfo inquired.

"I haven't seen him, my Lord," Gboyega answered.

The Kakanfo dismounted, landing in front of Master Gboyega. *"What?* Well, no time to deal with that now. Warriors…to the arena!"

CHAPTER 35

The Alaafin's spirits lifted upon seeing the real Aare Ona Kakanfo—led by Master Gboyega—descend into Ile Ogun.

"The Aare Ona Kakanfo!" The Alaafin said. "No doubt come to bring us news of a victory!"

The Aare Ona Kakanfo saluted the Alaafin as soon as his feet touched the floor of the arena. "Quite the opposite, I am afraid. We have suffered terrible losses at the hands of the Urabi, Your Highness. I—and three-quarters of the Eṣo—are all that remains of the armed forces of Oyo!"

The arena was filled with cries of shock, loss and despair.

"Citizens of Oyo, calm yourselves!" The Alaafin shouted. "I promise you that all will be well!"

"How did the war turn in favor of the Urabi?" Temileke asked. "Although their numbers are great, they are no match for our power."

"The Urabi are now led by two generals who possess powerful aṣe." The Kakanfo replied. "One is a witch they call Suffering's Bride. The other, a monster they call Jabbar, the Demon."

"They possess more aṣe than the Aare Ona Kakanfo of Oyo?" Temileke asked.

"A *bit* more," the Kakanfo replied. "And they approach Metropolitan Oyo as we speak. We must act quickly!"

"How long before they reach our walls?" The Alaafin asked.

"No later than tomorrow, at dawn, Your Highness," the Aare Ona Kakanfo replied.

A murmur spread throughout the arena.

"We have no time to *prepare!*" a middle-aged man, obviously a blacksmith by his calloused hands and old burn-scars that dotted his forearms, cried. "*All is lost!*"

"I am just a visitor…here with my children for the Grand Tournament!" a young woman sobbed. "How can you hope to protect us from the *Urabi?*"

Master Gboyega held up his hands and the murmuring diminished. "Citizens...guests...listen! Those soulless bastards will *never* breach our walls! Ogun—the great god of iron and war will—"

"Where was Ogun when our sons and daughters were dying at the hands of our enemy?!" An elderly man shouted, interrupting Master Gboyega.

Akin pushed past the Mino, who still surrounded him. The young man ran to his father's side. "Where was Ogun?

Where was *Ogun?*" He pounded his chest with his right fist. Right *here*, where he has always been!"

Akin pointed toward the ground between his feet. "And right here!" He then pointed toward the spectators in the bleachers. "And right *there*!"

The murmuring completely stopped as Akin commanded the attention of everyone in the arena.

"Warriors fought here today because a King called and we responded...and responded well," Akin continued. "Now, the *Urabi* call. They call for war...they call for death...they call for the destruction of our beliefs, our culture, our gods...and we—the greatest warriors to whom Onile has ever given birth—must respond in *kind*!"

Akin drew his swords. He pointed the sword in his left hand at the spectators, and the sword in his right hand at the competitors in the tournament. "Who among you will respond to the call of the Urabi? Who among you will stand and fight?"

Master Gboyega drew his twin iron swords. *"I* will fight!"

The competitors—Nkohbo, Bayo, Kondo and even Runihara—stood and shouted in unison: *"I* will fight!"

"No deals, this time, Bayo," Akin said.

"No deals," Bayo replied. "I was once a champion; a warrior. I fight to regain my honor...and a bit of glory!"

Akin nodded and smiled. "Welcome back, Brother!"

Oṣogbesan approached Akin slowly. He leered coldly at the Aare Ona Kakanfo for a brief moment and then placed a firm hand on Akin's shoulder. "I will fight, too!"

"I will stand with you also, son!"

Akin snapped his head toward his mother's voice. Oyabakin, now dressed in an indigo wrap skirt, blouse and gele, descended the ramp onto the main floor of the arena.

"As will *I!*" a voice shouted from the Royal Terrace.

Akin looked up. Şeeke stood at the edge of the Royal Terrace, looking down at Akin.

"Şeeke, no!" The Alaafin cried. I…I forbid it!"

"Baba, I am confused about some things that transpired here today," Şeeke said.

The princess redirected her gaze toward Akin. "And you *will* explain them to me! However, I *do* know that I love you."

"And I love you," Akin replied.

The murmuring began anew. Usiade gasped in shock.

Şeeke gazed at Akin longingly. Tears formed in her eyes as she continued to speak: "I also know that I am ready to fight—and, if I must, to *die*—by your side!"

"Şeeke…what? The Alaafin sobbed. "You cannot…"

"You are right, Your Highness!" Akin shouted. "Şeeke cannot!"

"What?" Şeeke asked. What do you mean, Akin?"

"Şeeke, you can*not* die by my side," Akin replied. "My *mother* cannot die by my side. My father…your brothers…these warriors… *none* of you can die by my side today…you won't have *time* to… because you we will be too busy *killing* Urabi dogs!"

Akin raised his swords high above his head. "Aşe?"

The spectators, warriors and even royalty raised their weapons or fists and the arena trembled from their response – "Aşe! Aşe! *Aşe!"*

CHAPTER 36

The Aare Ona Kakanfo stood upon the tall, earthen wall surrounding Metropolitan Oyo. He stared up at the red, pre-dawn sky and then perused the land beneath him.

In the distance, spanning as wide and as far as his eyes could see, was the Royal Orchard.

Bayo sprinted out of the Royal Orchard and approached the wall. "The trench has been dug around the wall as you ordered, sir!"

"Excellent," the Kakanfo replied. "The Urabi will be forced to come through the Royal Orchard and their steeds cannot maneuver through these dense trees. They will be forced to fight us on foot."

Akinkugbe, Eṣuṣeeke and Oṣogbesan approached the wall from the interior.

The warriors are ready, my Lord," Akin said.

"Good," the Kakanfo said. "What are our numbers?"

"The surviving Eṣo," Ṣeeke began. "The competitors from the Grand Tournament, the blacksmith, woodcarver and hunter guilds; the Emi Omo Eṣo, and even the Mino have volunteered their services."

"Excellent! The Mino are truly formidable. The ancestors favor us!" The Aare Ona Kakanfo said. "Akinkugbe, I need you up here with me!"

"Yes, sir!" Akin replied, as he bent his knees deeply.

Akin leapt upward, propelling himself a few feet above the wall. He landed without making a sound.

"Show off," Oṣogbesan whispered.

"Let's go see the Baṣorun," Ṣeeke said. He has a couple of things we need." The wizard and the princess dashed off toward the palace.

"Akin, I understand you posed as me in the Grand Tournament," the Aare Ona Kakanfo said sternly.

Akin turned his gaze from the Kakanfo and stared at the ground below. "Yes, my Lord."

"Look at me, warrior!" The Kakanfo commanded.

Akin turned his eyes toward the Kakanfo. "Yes, sir!"

"When this battle is won, you will pay for your crimes!" The Kakanfo exclaimed.

"Yes, my Lord." Akin replied.

"You will pay…in blood and sweat," the Aare Ona Kakanfo said. "As my Second-in Command!"

Akin raised an eyebrow. "Sir?"

"Akin, look around you," the Kakanfo said. "The people fight for *you*, not for Oyo…not for *me*."

"Sir, that is not true," Akin said, "You are…"

"*I* am motivated by law," the Aare Ona Kakanfo said, interrupting Akin. "You are motivated by *love*. We *will* win this day… not by the law over our heads, but by the love in our hearts."

CHAPTER 37

The army of Urabin marched to the mouth of the Royal Orchard. The ground shook from the synchronized stepping of heel and hoof. The fearsome force rode upon the backs of heavily armored camels that were bred for the harshness of war.

At the fore was Jabbar, the Demon, who rode upon a huge rhinoceros that was covered, from snout to tail, in bronze chainmail armor.

Jabbar wore a bronze helmet, with a large, bronze spike jutting from its crest, a bronze breastplate, and greaves and armbands—also of bronze. The Demon carried a monstrous war-hammer, constructed completely of white marble. The heavy maul was nearly the same hue as Jabbar's pallid flesh.

On Jabbar's right rode Suffering's Bride, in a litter that was balanced upon the backs of two camels tethered to it. The Bride wore a black, lace wedding dress, which started under her chin and ended at her ankles.

She wore the signature tan, curly-toe boots of the Al-Nur assassins, a black hijab head-dress and a tan niqab—a face mask that concealed all but Suffering's Bride's eyes from the lusts of men.

The Bride's eyes were so dark, the pupils were indistinguishable from the irises. Looking into Suffering's Bride's eyes felt like gazing into an endless abyss.

The Bride was armed with a whip made of braided camel hide and barbed with the talons of falcons.

On Jabbar's left rode the foppish eunuch, Jalili, who was dressed in a rose-colored suit of studded leather armor with a matching cape and suede boots.

Jalili rode upon a chariot that was pulled by four horses. The chariot was constructed of mahogany and trimmed in bronze.

"It is time to deliver our conditions," Jabbar said. "If they are not met to the letter, we will kill them all!"

* * *

On the opposite end of the Royal Orchard, the Aare Ona Kakanfo addressed the powerful force of warriors standing in ranks before him. A large, leather sack sat at his feet.

The aṣe of the Urabi army lies with Jabbar, the Demon and the witch, Suffering's Bride," the Kakanfo said. "It is time for me to meet with their Herald. Ṣeeke?"

"Yes, sir? Ṣeeke said, taking two steps forward from the regiment of warriors.

The Kakanfo picked up the leather sack. He pointed at the longbow slung across the princess's back and shoulder. "I pray that you are as good with that bow as your brothers, Tayewo and Kehinde, say."

Ṣeeke looked over her shoulder at her twin brothers, who stood in the ranks of warriors, and smiled. "I'm *better*, my Lord!"

"Good…we will need you to be," the Kakanfo replied. "The rest of you know what to do."

The Kakanfo strolled into the Royal Orchard with the large sack slung over his shoulder. It was time to come face-to-face with the Herald of the Urabi.

* * *

Jalili stepped down from his chariot and sashayed into the Royal Orchard.

"Warlord of Oyo," Jalili called. "The General of the Army of Urabin orders you and your army to lay down your weapons! Comply and none of you will be harmed."

The Aare Ona Kakanfo walked cautiously toward Jalili, stopping within ten paces of the obese Herald. The Kakanfo tossed the sack near Jalili's feet. The bag landed with a soft clink. "I am unarmed. We offer tribute to your Generals and to your Emir, asking that you leave in peace. No one has to die today."

"We accept your tribute," Jalili said. "But you are still ordered to lay down your weapons!"

The Kakanfo shook his head. "But, sir…"

"Lay down your weapons now," Jalili hissed. "Or we will stomp your people into wine!"

"Yes, sir," the Kakanfo replied.

The War Chief of War Chiefs peered over his left shoulder toward his warriors. "Your weapons…put them down!"

The Warriors of Oyo did not budge.

"Your weapons," the Kakanfo repeated. "Put them down, *now!*" Reluctantly, the warriors dropped their arms to the ground.

Jalili smiled triumphantly. He picked up the sack, threw it over his meaty shoulder and headed back toward the Urabi Army. The Aare Ona Kakanfo walked back toward the Warriors of Oyo.

"Tell your Emperor to prepare himself," Jalili called over his shoulder. "We want him on his knees, greeting us, when we arrive at the palace."

* * *

"It is done," Jalili crooned. The eunuch stood before the Army of Urabin gloating.

The men who made up the ranks of the Urabi Army had treated him less than amicably and did not regard him as a soldier—but as a perverse mockery of one. Now, he had proven them wrong. He had just negotiated the most important surrender in history *and* had received tribute from the Aare Ona Kakanfo, himself!

"What do you have there?" Jabbar asked, pointing a thick, chalky finger at the sack hanging from Jalili's shoulder.

Jalili poured gold coins from the sack onto the ground. The coins formed a small mound on the soft earth. Among the shimmering gold were tiny patches of dark brown. "A tribute from the infidels, sir," Jalili replied.

Jabbar pointed at the brown spots in the tiny mountain of coins. "And what is that? There…among the gold?"

Jalili squatted and reached into the mound, plucking out a palm seed from among the coins. "It is some type of seed, sir."

Jalili stood, inspecting the seed with his eyes, his nose and his fingers. "Strange people, these black-skinned savages of Onile. I suppose they use these seeds as another form of curr—"

The words died in Jalili's throat as a golden spear pierced the flesh behind his chin and tore through the top of his skull.

The seed in Jalili's hand had grown into a Seed-Warrior.

Soft flute music wafted through the Royal Orchard and the area surrounding it. The Urabi suddenly faced an army of Seed-Warriors—one warrior for each of the two hundred seeds in the sack. The gold had morphed into the Seed-Warriors' weapons.

"It is a *trap!*" Jabbar shouted. "The infidels use sorcery!"

Jalili collapsed. A waterfall of blood and pinkish-gray matter cascaded from the top of Jalili's skull, forming a crimson halo around the dead eunuch's head.

An inhuman, blood-chilling scream escaped Jabbar's twisted mouth as he swung his mighty war-hammer. Seed-Warrior after Seed-Warrior crumbled to dust under the destructive power of Jabbar's marble maul.

Suffering's Bride somersaulted from her litter, rending a Seed-Warrior in two, in mid-flip, with a crack of her whip.

The Urabi soldiers charged toward the Seed-Warriors ... and the Seed-Warriors met them, driving mystically enhanced golden spears through armor and into flesh...

* * *

On the opposite side of the Royal Orchard, the Warriors of Oyo picked up their weapons. Led by Bayo, they charged into the orchard toward the Urabi Army.

Akin, Master Gboyega, Mistress Oyabakin, Chief Oṣogbesan and the Aare Ona Kakanfo remained steadfast, near the wall. Ṣeeke stood upon the wall as well, armed with the magic longbow on loan to her from Temileke.

Another fetish, on loan from the Baṣorun lay at Ṣeeke's feet: the apere ayorunbo.

* * *

Bayo's punch struck an Urabi soldier in the nose. The Urabi's face collapsed around Bayo's gauntlet. The soldier fell to the ground, lifeless.

Another soldier screamed as Runihara tore through the man's left boot with his teeth and then gnawed off the soldier's toes.

Nkohbo crept up on Suffering's Bride as she fought a squad of Seed-Warriors. The Zulu giant grabbed the witch from behind, ensnaring her in a crushing bear-hug.

The bones in the Bride's ribcage, sternum and shoulder blades made a sickening, popping noise as she disjointed her torso.

Suffering's Bride's flaccid body slipped—serpent-like —from Nkohbo's grip. Nkohbo reached for the Bride's neck with his massive hands.

Suffering's Bride thrust outward with a back-kick, slamming her heel into Nkohbo's gut. The giant reeled backward, clutching at his aching belly.

Suffering's Bride slashed in a quick, upward, figure-eight pattern with her whip.

Nkohbo's left ear fell to the ground and bounced off into the Royal Orchard. His nose followed. His right ear and his cheek fell shortly after...The giant toppled over onto his belly. His breathing grew shallow, and then ceased.

Suffering's Bride stepped over Nkohbo's lifeless body en route to her next victim.

The mouth of the Royal Orchard soon became a gory mass of Onilean and Urabi flesh, sprinkled heavily with Seed-Warrior dust.

"Retreat!" Bayo screamed as he turned from the battle and sprinted into the Royal Orchard. "The Urabi will soon overwhelm us! *Retreat!*"

The surviving warriors on the side of Oyo broke away from the battle and followed Bayo.

A Captain of the Urabi Army pointed his sword toward the fleeing warriors. "The cowardly pups run! After them!"

"*Hold!*" Jabbar shouted, raising his war-hammer high above his head. "The black bastards are trying to spring another trap!"

The Urabi ended their pursuit of the Warriors of Oyo and stood fast at the mouth of the Royal Orchard.

* * *

"The Urabi are holding fast," Akin said, observing the army of Urabin from atop Oyo's earthen wall.

"Good," the Aare Ona Kakanfo replied. "Now, Şeeke! *Now!*"

Şeeke stared into the water that filled the apere ayorunbo. The image in the water was of the base of a tree at the mouth of the Royal Orchard. Poking out of the ground, near the tree's base, was an inch of reddish-brown detonation cord.

The princess drew an arrow from the quiver on her back. As soon as the broad arrowhead touched the air, it burst into flames.

Şeeke strung the flaming arrow on her bow and then pulled the bowstring past her right ear. The princess aimed the arrow at the water in the apere ayorunbo, and then released the bowstring.

The flaming arrow sliced through the water and then disappeared.

* * *

At the mouth of the Royal Orchard, the sky ripped open and the flaming arrow flew through the jagged wound.

Ṣeeke's aim was true. The arrow struck the camouflaged detonation cord.

The lit fuse hissed in protest.

Suffering's Bride noticed the cord first. Under the witch's niqab, her eyes widened in shock.

Possessing no tongue with which to scream, the Bride pointed at the detonation cord, shaking her index finger at the burning fuse in order to draw attention to it.

Jabbar followed the Bride's finger to the fuse, which had nearly reached the base of a huge palm tree. "Retreat! The infidels have deceived us! Run! *Now!*"

Jabbar, the Demon, Suffering's Bride and fifty Urabi soldiers fled from the Royal Orchard. The rest of the Urabi were locked in battle with the Seed-Warriors or struggling to move through the sea of the dead and the dying.

A massive explosion erupted from the palm tree. The tree shattered into thousands of sharp, pointed splinters that impaled and shredded Urabi flesh. A moment later, the Urabi were engulfed in flames and billowing clouds of black smoke.

A second flaming arrow burst through the tear in the sky and hit another fuse at the Urabi's right flank. The second explosion that followed—even larger than the first—rocked the mouth of the Royal Orchard.

Screams of terror and pain rose from the battered, bloodied and burned Urabi.

* * *

The Aare Ona Kakanfo pointed the Invincible Staff toward grisly scene at the mouth of the Royal Orchard. "Attack while they are disoriented! Master Gboyega…Mistress Oyabakin….Suffering's Bride is yours! Akin and I will deal with the Demon!"

As the Warriors of Oyo charged toward the stunned Urabi, Ṣeeke rapidly fired swarms of arrows into the apere ayorunbo. Scores of Urabi soldiers fell as arrows rained from a crack in the sky.

The warriors on the side of Oyo descended upon the Urabi, dispatching them with sword and spear and staff.

Oṣogbesan played a staccato tune on his flute. The roots of the trees in the Royal Orchard sprang to life, writhing and lashing like the tentacles of an enraged, giant squid.

A network of roots shot up from the ground, impaling the feet of several Urabi soldiers. The Urabi fell to the ground, wailing in anguish.

Roots wrapped around the legs of Urabi and then snatched them into the earth—their screams, muffling, as their heads sank beneath the soil...

* * *

Jabbar shook off the stunning effects of the explosions.

A Mino Warrior leapt toward Jabbar, the Demon, her sword raised to deliver a decapitating slash.

As clarity returned, Jabbar's rhinoceros steed seemed to gain focus; to become more alert.

The rhinoceros thrust its head upward, piercing the Mino's breastplate with its wicked horn. The Mino coughed up a clot of blood and flesh as the rhino gored her belly—tearing through muscles and entrails.

The albino rhinoceros hoisted the Mino Warrior up toward its master.

Jabbar, the Demon swung his war-hammer in a downward arc.

The maul struck the Mino's helmet with a loud crack. A moment later, the Mino's head and helmet disappeared into her shoulders. A crimson mist filled the air and the Mino went limp.

The rhinoceros shook its large head, sending the Mino's headless body flying across the Royal Orchard.

* * *

Master Gboyega and Mistress Oyabakin stood over Suffering's Bride, who pulled herself to her feet and then shook off the disorientation wrought by the explosion.

"We could have killed you while you lay there vulnerable," Master Gboyega said.

"But where would have been the fun in that?" Mistress Oyabakin chimed in with a shrug.

The Bride swung her whip in reply. The barbed weapon traveled in a wide arc toward the masters' torsi,
    whistling as it carved a swath through the air.

Oyabakin leapt into the air, cartwheeling over the lethal strike.

Master Gboyega crouched low, allowing the whip to fly harmlessly over his head.

Oyabakin drove her left fist into the Bride's face. The witch's tan niqab turned a moist dark brown as her face collapsed around Mistress Oyabakin's fist.

Suffering's Bride flicked her wrist and her whip came to life, wrapping itself around Oyabakin's punching arm.

The Bride leapt backward, pulling the whip taut. The falcon talons dug into the flesh of Mistress Oyabakin's forearm, shredding the muscles and nerve endings.

Master Gboyega slashed upward into the Bride's whip with his left sword while thrusting his right sword into the witch's abdomen.

The whip loosened its hold on Mistress Oyabakin's arm as Master Gboyega's keen blade cleaved the weapon in two. Mistress

Oyabakin's wounded arm fell limply against her thigh.

Suffering's Bride stumbled backward, clutching at the gaping gash in her belly.

Mistress Oyabakin exploded upward and forward, striking Suffering's Bride in the side of her neck with a
crushing right knee.

The witch's head bent toward Mistress Oyabakin's knee at an odd angle, her left ear nearly touching her shoulder-blade. The Bride fell onto her face, lifeless.

Mistress Oyabakin stared down at the corpse of the Bride. Her lips curled upward into a wry smile. "Suffering is now a widower."

* * *

Jabbar, the Demon drove his heels into his steed's side. The massive, white rhinoceros charged forward into the Royal Orchard, reducing the trees in its path to splinters and dust.

The albino creature quickly advanced toward Akin and the Aare Ona Kakanfo, who stood defiantly deep within the orchard. The Kakanfo and Akin rushed to meet the monstrous beast and its master.

The Aare Ona Kakanfo hurled the Invincible Staff. The ancient, magic weapon glowed an intense indigo as it sped towards the rhinoceros's thick, alabaster, left foreleg.

Akin slashed at the rhino's right foreleg with his ironwood swords. Both of the creature's forelegs shattered at the knee.

The beast let loose a sickening wail as its front legs collapsed inward.

The rhinoceros's chest slammed to the ground, kicking up a cloud of dirt and blood as its momentum continued to carry it forward. The Demon tumbled off the rhino's back and then disappeared within the earthen fog.

Oṣogbesan played a joyous tune on his flute as he danced in the Royal Orchard: "*Jabbar and his foul beast are defeated*," the wizard sang. "*Suffering's Bride lies dead and the Urabi dogs are vanquished!*"

The warriors of Oyo joined Oşogbesan in celebration, singing and dancing in victory. "*Jabbar and his foul beast are defeated. Suffering's Bride lies dead and the Urabi dogs are vanquished!*"

The Aare Ona Kakanfo's eyes—enhanced by the magic of the Invincible Staff—spotted movement in the thick, billowing cloud of dirt behind Oşogbesan.

Suddenly, Jabbar rose out of the cloud, his war-hammer raised high. An expression of mindless rage was spread across the Demon's face as it leapt toward the unsuspecting wizard.

The Kakanfo's shoulder rammed Oşogbesan's chest, knocking the wizard out of the path of Jabbar's fierce attack.

Jabbar's maul slammed down onto the Aare Ona Kakanfo's back, nearly folding him in half. A gush of blood spewed from the Aare Ona Kakanfo's mouth as he collapsed.

An arrow shot across the Orchard, piercing Jabbar's right triceps. The war-hammer fell from Jabbar's hands and struck the ground with a loud thud.

A second arrow struck Jabbar's right calf.

The Demon dropped to his knees.

Şeeke ran across the orchard toward Jabbar, firing a volley of arrows.

Each arrow found its mark, piercing Jabbar's breastplate— impaling the monster's bladder, liver, lungs and heart. Jabbar convulsed violently, but his eyes remained focused and full of rage.

Akin leapt toward Jabbar, landing a few inches in front of him. Akin grabbed the rim of Jabbar's helmet with both hands and then snatched the spiked helmet off of the Demon's head.

Akinkugbe swung the top of the helmet toward Jabbar's face. The large spike atop the helmet pierced Jabbar's forehead and then punched through the back of the Demon's skull.

Jabbar sat back limply on his heels. His arms dangled at his sides and his head flopped backward. The Demon's eyes rolled back in his head and his jaw fell slack.

A moment later, a hissing death rattle escaped the Demon's

gaping maw and then he was no more.

The few surviving Urabi soldiers—less than a score total—fled the Royal Orchard, with the Eṣo in hot pursuit.

CHAPTER 38

Akin knelt beside the Aare Ona Kakanfo, cradling the Warlord of Warlord's head in his arms. "Warriors, gather around! The Aare Ona Kakanfo wishes to speak!"

The warriors on the side of the Oyo Empire sauntered over. For those too injured to walk, their brethren carried them. All took a knee around Akin and the Aare Ona Kakanfo.

Akin raised the Kakanfo's head, allowing the leader to see his troops.

"You fought well this day, warriors," The Kakanfo said. "Celebrate this victory, but stay forever vigilant, for the Urabi will one day return!"

"We will, my Lord," Master Gboyega said.

"And please, citizens of Oyo…stay united," the Aare Ona Kakanfo continued. "United under your *new* Aare Ona Kakanfo… Master Gboyega Ogunlade! *Never* has there been a warrior more worthy! Aṣe?!"

The warriors of Oyo and from allied lands responded with a resounding: "Aṣe! Aṣe! Aṣe!"

"Let everyone know too that the son of our Aare Ona Kakanfo is, himself, now a Balogun and Second-In-Command to his father!" Kakanfo Ibikunle commanded.

"Aṣe! Aṣe! Aṣe!" the warriors shouted once more.

The Aare Ona Kakanfo looked up into Master Gboyega's eyes and smiled weakly. "Now, my Lord, I humbly ask your permission to join my Ancestors with *honor*."

Master Gboyega looked away from the former Aare Ona Kakanfo. Tears rolled down the old War-Master's cheeks. "Permission granted, mighty warrior of Oyo. Rest well!"

The former Aare Ona Kakanfo smiled, closed his eyes and fell into eternal sleep.

CHAPTER 39

Akin held Ṣeeke's hand as they escorted Oṣogbesan to the gates leading from Metropolitan Oyo. "Are you sure we cannot convince you to stay longer, my friend?" Akin asked.

"My apologies, War Chief, but I have nearly spent a full moon here already and I am missing my little village," Oṣogbesan replied.

"But you *will* return for the wedding?" Ṣeeke inquired.

"I would not dare miss it, Your Majesty," Oṣogbesan answered. "Of course, had the Grand Tournament not been…interrupted, it would be *me* you are marrying, not Akin."

"Please," Akin chuckled. "I would have beaten you as badly as Abe beat Bayo upon his return to Oyo!"

"Perhaps you should have your mother examine you," Oṣogbesan said. "For I fear you have lost your senses."

Akin smiled slyly as he drew the ironwood swords from his back. "Then, please, help me *find* them, wizard!"

"As you command, my Lord," Oṣogbesan said as he tossed a handful of palm seeds into the air. "As you command,...!"

THE END

ONCE UPON A TIME IN AFRIKA
GLOSSARY

1. PEOPLE

Aare Ona Kakanfo [ah-AH-ray O-na kah-KAH-en-FO]: *War Chief of War Chiefs; Leader of the Eşo*

Abe [ah-BAY]: *Herald of the Aare Ona Kakanfo; a Balogun and a Senior Officer of the Eşo*

Ajoke [ah-JO-keh]: *The Alaafin's fourth wife; Mother of Tayewo and Kehinde*

Akin [ah-KEEN]: *Short for Akinkugbe*

Akinkugbe [ah-KEEN-koog-bay]: *Young warrior who enters the Grand Tournament under the guise of the Aare Ona Kakanfo*

Alaafin [ah-LAH-ah-FEEN]: *"Owner of the palace;" Emperor of the Oyo Empire*

Baale [BAH-lay]: *Town or village chief*

Baba [bah-BAH]: *"Father"* or [BAH-bah]: *"Male priest"*

Baba Fafore [BAH-bah FAH-faw-ray]: *Royal diviner*

Balogun [bah-LO-goon]: *War Chief*

Bamgbala [bahm-BAH-lah]: *The Gorilla-Warrior*

Başorun [bah-sho-ROON]: *Prime Minister*

Bayo [BY-yaw]: *Former wrestling champion of Ajaland*

Chitauri [chee-tah-OO-ree]: *Malevolent race of reptile-men*

Efunlade [eh-FOON-lah-DAY]: *Akin's maternal grandmother; "White Warrior" of Oyo legend*

Emi Omo Eşo [ay-MI aw-maw AY-sho]: *Young warriors who train to become Eşo*

Emir [ay-MEER]: *Ruler of Urabin*

Eşo [AY-sho]: *Elite warriors of the Oyo Empire; comprised totally of Balogun*

Eşuşeeke [ay-shoo-SHAY-keh]: *Daughter of the Alaafin; warrior and master archer*

Fakoya [FAH-kaw-YAH]: *Akin's maternal grandfather*

Fet Bin Fet [feht-bin-FEHT]: *Shekhem of Kamet*

Gboyega Ogunlade [BO-yay-GAH o-GOON-lah-DAY]: *Akin's father; Master teacher of the Emi Omo Eşo*

Hashashin [hah-SHAH-sheen]: *Initiates of the Al-Nur Assassin's Guild*

Hausa [HOW-sa]: *Onilean ethnic group that allies with Urabi*

Ibikunle Şangodele [EE-bee-KOON-lay shahn-GO-day-lay]: *Current Aare Ona Kakanfo*

Ikeade [ee-KEH-ah-DAY]: *Royal Chef*

Iya [EE-yah]: *Mother or female priest*

Jabbar [juh-BAHR]: *"The Demon;" ruthless mercenary; former general of the armed forces of Urabin*

Jagun-jagun [JAH-goon-JAH-goon]: *Warrior*

Jalili [juh-LEE-lee]: *Eunuch; mercenary; Jabbar's partner*

Kehinde [KEH-heen-DAY]: *Şeeke's brother; Tayewo's twin*

Kentake Amanikhete [KEHN-ta-KAY ah-MAHN-ee-KEH-tay]: *Warrior-King of Kas (female)*

Kondo [kon-DO]: *Greatest wrestler of Kas*

Maasai [mah-SY]: *Onilean ethnic group*

Maasai Moran [mah-SY mo-RAHN]: *Maasai Warrior*

Mino [mee-NAW]: *Famed and feared Onilean women warriors*

Nangwaya [nahn-GWY-ah]: *Greatest of the Maasai Moran*

Nkohbo Busisiwe [uhn-KO-bo BOO-see-SEE-way]: *Famed giant Zulu warrior*

Nkonkoni [uhn-kon-KON-nee]: *Nkohbo's umama (mother)*
Oba [AW-bah]: *King*

Omobe [aw-MAW-bay]: *The Wrestler with a Thousand Scars*

Oşabiyi [O-shah-BEE-yee]: *Akin's paternal grandmother; commissioned the creation of the Royal Orchard*

Oşogbesan [o-SHOG-beh-SAHN]: *Baale of Ijeti; powerful wizard*

Oyabakin [AW-yah-BAH-keen]: *Akin's mother; recognized as the greatest fighter on the continent of Onile*

Oyo Mesi [aw-YAW MAY-see]: *The seven rulers of the Oyo Empire;*

members of the Royal Court, headed by the Başorun

Rogba Adewale [RAWG-bah ah-DAY-wah-LAY]: *Alaafin of Oyo*

Runihara [ROO-nee-HAH-rah]: *Feared khoisan (pygmy)-warrior*

Şeeke [SHAY-keh]: *Short for Eşuşeeke*

Shekhem [SHEH-kum]: *Ruler of Kamet; "Pharaoh"*

Tayewo [tah-YAY-wo]: *Şeeke's brother; Kehinde's twin*

Temileke [TAY-mee-LAY-kay]: *The Başorun of the Oyo Empire*

Temilola [TAY-mee-lo-LAH]: *The Alaafin's third wife*

Toki [TO-kee]: *Bayo's wife*

Umama [OO-mah-mah]: *Mother*

Urabi [oo-RAH-bee]: *Desert-dwelling Ethnic group of conquerors from the nation of Urabin*

Usiade [OO-see-ah-DAY]: *The Alaafin's Great Wife; Şeeke's mother*

Winlawe [ween-LAH-weh]: *The Alaafin's second wife*

2. PLACES

Ajaland [AH-jah-land]: *One of the seven layers of Oyo*

Apanakoti [ah-pah-nah-KO-tee]: *One of the seven continents*

Butulozabwei [BOO-too-lo-ZAHB-way]: *Southernmost nation on the continent of Onile*

Celtshire [KEHLT-shir]: *One of the seven continents*

Hapi [HAH-pee]: *The longest river in the world*

Hoostheim [HOOST-hym]: *One of the seven continents*

Huan Chuan [hwahn-CHWAHN]: *Nation located in the east of Sighashri*

Ifonyin [ee-FON-yeen]: *Nation in the Ajaland layer of the Oyo Empire*

Igbo Bamiṣo [eeg-BO BAH-mee-sho]: *"Forest of the Bamiṣo Clan;" a magical—and dangerous—forest ruled by a mischievous family of Iwin*

Ijeti [ee-JEH-tee]: *Small farming village; Oṣogbesan is the Baale*

Ile Aje [EE-lay ah-JEH]: *"City of Witches"*

Ile Ogun [EE_lay o-GOON]: *"Home of Ogun;" arena where Grand Tournament is held*

Inkmehez [eenk-meh-HEHS]: *One of the seven continents*

Kamet [KAH-meht]: *Nation in the northeast of Onile; a beautiful land of mystery and magic*

Kas [KAHS]: *Easternmost nation of Onile; Kamet's predecessor; home to the oldest university on the planet*

Kirinyaga [KEE-reen-YAH-gah]: *Eastern nation of Onile*

Kongo [KON-go]: *Nation located in central Onile*

Ma-Iti [mah-ee-TEE]: *Nation located in the Southlands of Sighashri*

Matongpa [mah-TONG-pa]: *One of the seven continents*

Oja-oba [O-jah-AW-bah]: *"The King's Market;" vast, Royal*

Marketplace in Metropolitan Oyo

Oke Itase [O-kay ee-TAH-say]: *Tallest hill in the world; once inhabited by the legendary White Warrior*

Onile [o-NEE-lay]: *The wealthiest and most culturally advanced of the seven continents; ancestral home of all humans*

Oyo [aw-YAW]: *The longest standing and most powerful empire on the planet*

Padampong [PAH-dahm-PONG]: *Nation located in the east of Sighashri*

Qanas [kah-NAHS]: *Nation located in the Southlands of Sighashri*

Quraish [koo-RYSH]: *Capital of Urabin*

Sighashri [see-GAHSH-ree]: *One of the seven continents*

Urabin [oo-rah-BEEN]: *Nation located in the Southlands of Sighashri*

Vashti-Shah [VAHSH-tee-SHAH]: *Nation located in the Southlands of Sighashri*

Yojinaga [YO-jee-NAH-gah]: *Nation located in the east of Sighashri*

3. THINGS

Apere ayorunbo [ah-PEH-reh AH-yo-ROON-bo]: *Magic fetish that allows user to teleport to other lands / dimensions*

Aṣe [ah-SHEH]: *Life force; power and authority given through command of said life force*

Awon Iyawa [ah-WAWN EE-yah-WAH] *"Our Mothers;" witches; powerful, revered and feared spiritual beings that are the embodiment of primal female energy*

Bamişo [BAH-mee-sho]: *A mischievous clan of Iwin*

Bata [BAH-tah]: *A sacred trio of drums used to invoke spirits and control emotions*

Buba [BOO-bah]: *Blouse or shirt*

Egusi [ay-GOO-see]: *Delicious soup popular throughout Onile*

Enkang [EHN-kahng]: *Circular fence constructed from acacia tree; protects Maasai village*

Eşu [ay-SHOO]: *Orişa of law-enforcement; truth and the Divine Messenger; Divine Trickster; keeper of aşe; General of the negative forces*

Garugu [gah-ROO-goo]: *Powerful, metal eating dragon that once terrorized Oyo*

Ha-Kri [hah-KREE]: *A monstrous creature with half-a-body*

Hagagah [HAH-ga-ga]: *Lord of the Kpelekpe*

Ifa [ee-FAH]: *System of divination; knowledge, wisdom and understanding contained in the 256 Odu Ifa*

Iginla [EE-gee-ehn-LA]: *"The Big Tree;" massive, ancient, divine tree considered to be mother of all trees*

Inkajijik [een-KAH-jee-jeek]: *Maasai houses*

Irosun Meji [ee-RO-soon MEH-jee]: *One of the 256 containers of knowledge, wisdom and understanding called Odu Ifa*

Iwin [ee-WEEN]: *Fairies that inhabit some forests in Onile*

Kini [KEE-nee]: *Bayo's horse*

Kpelekpe [kuh-PAY-lehk-PAY]: *Race of Were-hyena*

Munujuniq [MOO-noo-JOO-neek]: *Urabi artillery weapon; a trebuchet (type of catapult)*

Nkulukulu [ehn-KOO-loo-KOO-loo]: *Zulu name for the Creator*

Obatala [aw-bah-TAH-lah]: *Oriṣa of whiteness, light, clarity, cleanliness, intelligence and humor; Eldest Oriṣa*

Odu [o-DOO]: *256 containers that hold knowledge, wisdom and understanding; the patterns of life (also called "Odu Ifa")*

Ogun [o-GOON]: *Oriṣa of Iron, War and the Arts*

Olodumare [o-LO-doo-MAH-ray]: *The Supreme Being; Creator*

Opele [o-PEH-leh]: *Divining chain used to determine which Odu apply to the life of the person divined for*

Oriṣa [o-REE-shah]: *Spirit or deity that reflects one of the manifestations of Olodumare; Force of Nature*

Oṣoosi [o-SHO-see]: *Oriṣa of the hunt, archery and swift justice*

Oṣun [aw-SHOON]: *Oriṣa of beauty, love and intimacy*

Oya [aw-YAH]: *Oriṣa of wind (incl. hurricanes and tornadoes) and quick change; leads her husband, Ṣango, into battle*

Ṣango [shahn-GO]: *Oriṣa of thunder and lightning; third Alaafin of Oyo*

Ṣekere [SHEH-keh-REH]: *Instrument consisting of a dried gourd with beads woven into a net covering the gourd; it is shaken and/or hit against the hands*

Shuka [SHOO-kah]: *The red-colored robe worn exclusively by Maasai warriors*

Şokoto [SHO-ko-to]: *Trousers, esp. the shin-length ones worn by warriors*

Yaba Yinka [YAH-bah YEEN-kah]: *Leader of the Red Order of Awon Iyawa*

4. GREETINGS / COMMANDS

A dupe [ah-DOO-pay]: *"We thank you"*

Dide [DEE-day]: *"Rise"*

Ekaale [eh-KAH-lay]: *"Good afternoon"*

Ekaaro [eh-KAH-ro]: *"Good morning"*

Ekurole [eh-KOO-ro-leh]: *"Good evening"*

Ko tope [ko-TO-pay]: *"You're welcome"*

Mo dupe [mo-DOO-pay]: *"I thank you"*

Odabo [o-DAH-bo]: *"See you later"*

Oto [o-TO]: *"Stop"*

Us-sulum Ulokam [oos-soo-LOOM oo-LO-kahm]: *"Peace be unto you"*

Wu-Ulokam sulum [woo-oo-LO-kahm soo-LOOM]: *"Unto you be peace also"*

CHANGA'S SAFARI

A Sword and Soul Adventure by Milton J. Davis

Take an
adventure like
you've never
imagined.

On Sale Now!

Fourteen Writers. Fourteen Artists.
One Unforgettable Anthology

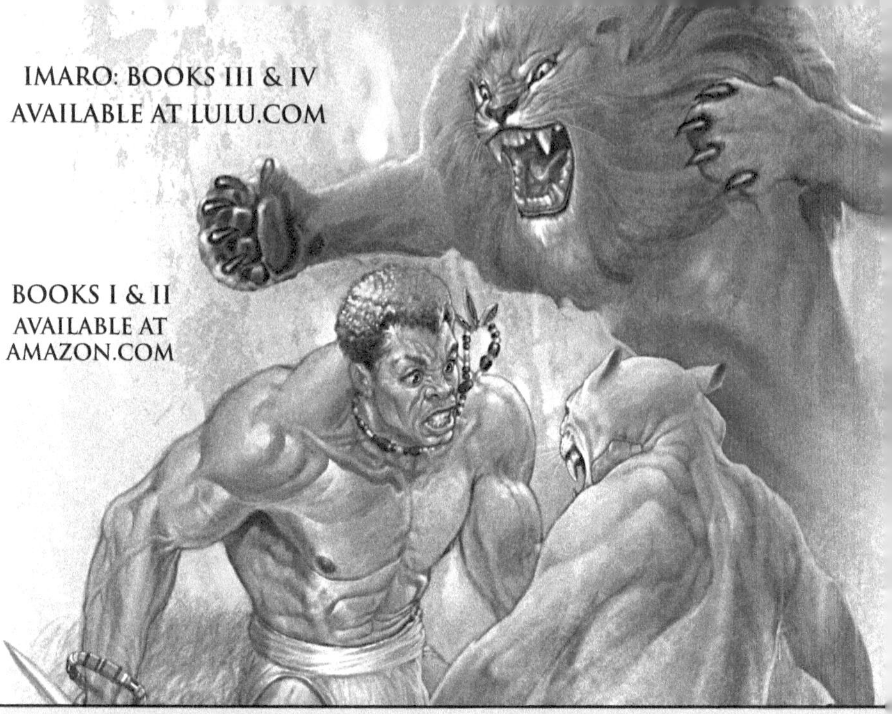

IMARO: BOOKS III & IV
AVAILABLE AT LULU.COM

BOOKS I & II
AVAILABLE AT
AMAZON.COM

CHARLES R. SAUNDERS

FATHER OF SWORD AND SOUL

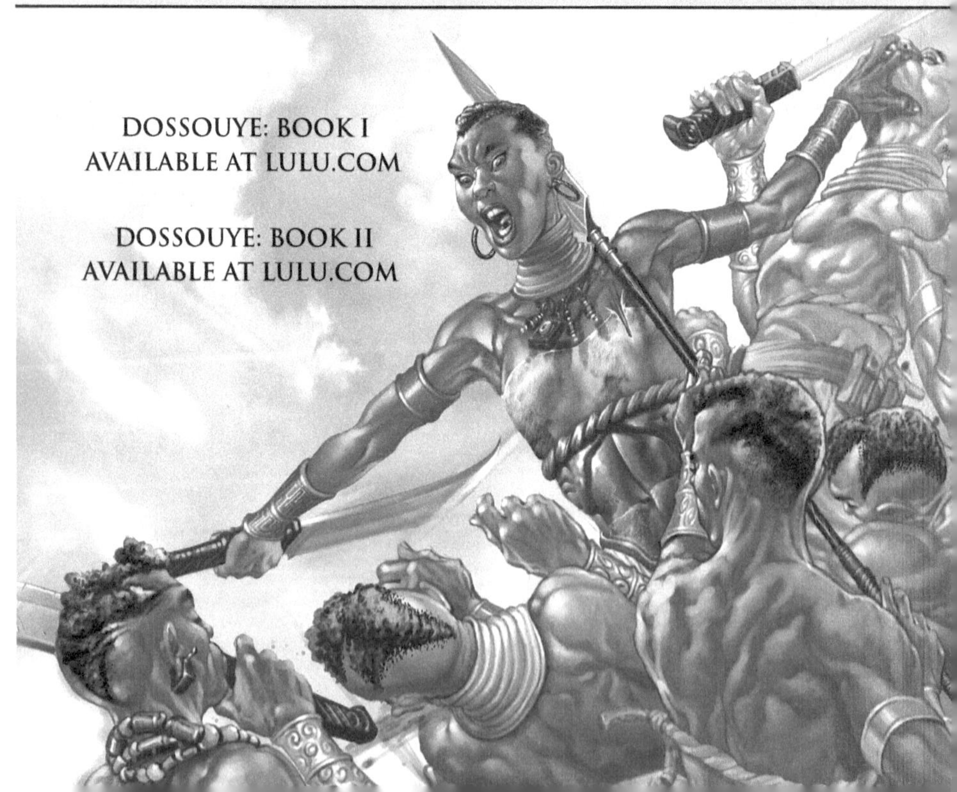

DOSSOUYE: BOOK I
AVAILABLE AT LULU.COM

DOSSOUYE: BOOK II
AVAILABLE AT LULU.COM

www.ingramcontent.com/pod-product-compliance
Lightning Source LLC
Chambersburg PA
CBHW052141170626
46812CB00004B/1529

* 9 7 8 0 9 8 0 0 8 4 2 3 8 *